michele.abramoff@orange.fr

ISBN 979-10-91423-14-4

Michèle Abramoff

MISS JENSEN
AND HER LABRADOR

A Detective Novel

Translated from the French by Linda Campbell

Miss Jensen And Her Labrador

CHAPTER 1.

Paula rang insistently one last time, before giving up and looking for her keys. As she rummaged through her bag, she took a few steps back and once more looked up at the façade of the building in front of her: all its lights were switched off. Nor was there any light coming from the wing of the house where Martine, her sister lived, and her car wasn't in the courtyard. Paula had called her two days earlier to let her know that she was coming, and she'd said that she would wait up for her. They had chatted for a long time over the telephone, excited by the prospect of spending a whole weekend together.

The moment that she turned the key in the lock, Paula felt her heart start to race. Ridiculous. Normally she wasn't easily scared, not the type to be unsettled. Quite the opposite, in fact - she was known as someone who was calm and in control of herself.

A cool head, people would say.

She pushed open the door and breathed in the bitter-sweet odour of wax which lingered in the hallway. Mrs Perreira had cleaned the house the previous day. Usually, Mrs Perreira only worked in Boyrive on Tuesday mornings, but whenever Paula telephoned to say that she would be coming to spend the weekend, on her own or with her husband, the cleaning-lady would always come back on Thursdays to air the rooms and make up the beds, and would come back again on Saturday mornings to prepare the meals. Furthermore, since Paula's sister had settled in the wing of the house three months ago, Mrs Perreira also cleaned for her for two hours on Tuesday afternoons. It was the absolute minimum needed since the house was so big, and really it could have done with more to take care of the ground-floor and the ten bedrooms of the main part of the building, in addition to the eight rooms of the wing – even if the new occupant barely used half of them.

Paula flicked a switch, turning on several lights at once. On her left, the double doors were wide open, leading to two adjoining reception rooms. On her right, the door that led to the study was closed. She opened it a fraction and peered in. Everything was tidy and without a speck of dust, the solid mahogany furniture - not varnished but waxed - glinted slightly. The room had remained exactly as her father had left it: on the study table lay the letter rack overflowing with envelopes, the ink-stained blotting roller, the silver paper-cutter left on top of a philatelic journal (with his sedentary job, antique colonial furniture and stamp-collecting were his own way of travelling the world), and everything gave the impression that time had stood still.

Paula and Martine had lost their parents ten years earlier in a plane accident. It had happened in May while they were returning from a fortnight's holiday in Guadeloupe. Their daughters had been getting ready to meet them at Roissy airport; their arrival was planned for ten past four. That day, however, on the one o'clock news the TV presenter announced, in that particular manner at once grave and eager that all journalists have when reporting catastrophes, that the plane coming from Pointe à-Pitre had crashed a few minutes after take-off. All the passengers on board the Airbus, all two hundred and forty of them, along with the seven crew members, had died. The plane had come down forty miles from the coast, and had sunk to a depth of seven hundred metres. It had exploded upon impact with the water, and all hope of recovering the bodies was lost. This cold, informative delivery of the news of their parents' death was, especially for such young girls, particularly brutal.

They couldn't even bury them as they were lost in the ocean along with hundreds of their fellow travellers. Paula eventually resigned herself to the thought that it was, actually, the most fitting resting place for them, since the whole of mankind came from the ocean millions of years ago, and each time she saw the sea, she thought of them. Three days later, a postcard arrived in the mail from La Désirade, a picture of a beautiful sunset over the Atlantic: "We're having a wonderful holiday! Lots of love, see you soon."

Overnight, the two sisters found themselves alone in the world. Paula was twenty and her sibling had just turned eighteen, which had spared them the formalities of guardianship. Fortunately, their parents hadn't left them penniless. Their father, Director of Client Management at a major bank, had proved apt at managing the family inheritance. Upon opening the wills, the solicitor read the terms with a soft, approving smile. A bourgeois fortune, built piece by piece over the years, is particularly pleasing to solicitors: it conveys a moral and aesthetic pleasure, like a work of art whose creation is the work of decades.

To begin with, there was the apartment in Paris: three hundred meters square, on Saint-Dominique road, which the bank had agreed to mortgage at a very favourable rate and which was almost completely repaid. Their parents were joint equal owners. ("It's quite amusing," the solicitor had remarked with a grey-wigged air of sagacity, forgetting that he was talking to young girls who had only recently been orphaned, "how people get married under a law that demands a total separation of goods, and yet they buy everything together...")

From their father, they had been left his entire portfolio of stocks and shares, mostly comprised of shares of a little-known business dealing in tools and machinery, which was, however, a leader in the market: the dividends alone would have been enough to support his two daughters. There was also a lump sum of money that had been accumulating over the years in a savings account.

From their mother, continued the solicitor, savouring each item as if it were a dainty morsel, there was the house in Boyrive, which she in turn had inherited from her parents: a seventeenth-century building in excellent condition, set in an estate of five acres, with all its rich furnishings – some of which were beautiful bourgeois eighteenth-century pieces destined to increase in value – and eleven paintings of the Barbizon school. There was also some money in bonds and treasury bills, and some fine jewellery.

Of course, their parents had life insurance which, being tax exempt, came to two large, immediately-available amounts. The solicitor knew nothing about the money in the Zurich account, the interest of which had been paying for the family's winter holidays in Davos and Gstaadt for two decades: on this, the wills were silent.

Leaving the office, Paula and Martine headed to a café and sat down. They stayed still for a moment, silent and stunned. Until then, they had never been very bothered about money, and now, surprised to find themselves so young and so rich, they smiled with embarrassment, torn between grief (which had pulled back after the first blow but never failed to rush back in) and an acute sense of freedom.

To add to their riches, the two sisters were also beautiful, beauty being in and of itself a kind of capital (one which can also be squandered). Their mother, who had never been pretty but did not lack a sense of humour, loved to recount how she had always promised herself when she was quite young that she would marry a handsome man to ensure a better genetic legacy. She had set her sights on a tall blond whom she had met at tennis, a boy of Danish origin called Christian Jensen. He was blessed with magnificent grey eyes, a warm smile and a straight hand-shake – qualities equally appreciated by the bank where her parents had found him a position. And voilà! The two girls resembled their father: two slim clear-complexioned blonds, with eyes that changed colour from blue to grey, with open, harmonious faces, though their noses were a little short (as for their personalities, they were like day and night). Having given each other what they hoped for, their parents got along well, and the little ones grew up in a happy home.

Paula went straight to the kitchen, a large room with two steps leading down into it, where the house's inhabitants would naturally converge. Evoking the cosy farm kitchens of long ago, it provided the refuge of a warm den in winter and a welcome freshness in summer. Paula thought she might find a note there: Martine, a painter, usually left any notes in the middle of the table under a brightly-coloured water jug that immediately attracted one's attention. The expanse of the table was, however, completely bare. Disappointed, she listened to her phone's voicemail and walked over to the telephone hung on the wall to check there was a dial tone. She told herself to be patient: Martine had, no doubt, been unexpectedly called somewhere and would appear shortly.

A half-empty bottle of wine stood on the sideboard. Paula poured herself a glass and set about examining the letters that she had pulled out of the box in passing. Addressed to her were only adverts and bills. Two letters were addressed to her sister; they both had a postmark but it was only possible to hazard a guess as to when they had arrived. The only certainty was that Martine hadn't picked up the post that morning.

The kitchen clock chimed eleven. Normally, at that time, they would have been sat at the table with a glass of wine, chatting quietly together. They always enjoyed meeting up, even if after two days they got on each other's nerves, one with her unpredictability, forgetfulness and her inability to manage her life, and the other with her protective attitude, the authoritative tone that she sometimes used in spite of herself, since being the elder child she felt the burden of responsibility after the death of their parents.

Paula looked around the room with its large oak dresser, the sculpted sideboard, the enormous thirty-year old American refrigerator that purred intermittently as its whole frame vibrated, the pale yellow walls, the paint peeling in places. A mixture of anguish and nostalgia washed over her. They had had such good times in this kitchen, with their grandparents who would take care of them for a month during the summer holidays when they were little (they had also died, a few months apart from each other, four years before the plane crash that had taken the life of their daughter). Later on, they would invite friends over for a weekend when their grandmother gave them the run of the house. At that time, the tennis court was well-kept, there was water in the swimming pool, and they had no end of friends: sometimes there were about twenty of them around the table, squeezed in like sardines.

Paula also used to enjoy having a meal there with her husband. Arriving on a Friday night, André would open a bottle of Margaux or, if the weather was warm, a crisp Chardonnay. They would sit down to a ready-meal that they'd picked up from Lenôtre on the way out of Paris, and that Paula only needed to reheat in the microwave. "This is the life…" André would say, happy to forget work for two days. That was, however, at the beginning of their married life; he didn't often accompany his wife these days.

Time stretched on, and the phones remained silent. Paula called her sister's mobile, only getting through to her voicemail. She left a message asking her to call, trying not to betray her anxiety.

The only thing left to do was to check Martine's apartment. Paula thought about it for a moment, but a sort of apprehension held her back. She reasoned with herself that Martine's car wasn't there, nor her dog César, whom she adored and who followed her around. Everything suggested that Martine had had to leave in a hurry.

Paula left the kitchen through the back door in order to glance over the back of the house. It was a splendid, clear end-of-summer evening, with a light breeze that stirred the leaves of the weeping willow and rippled through the grass of the lawn that drifted gently down to the Essonne river. She noted that the terrace furniture hadn't been brought in, the chairs were simply folded and the parasols closed, but there was nothing surprising about that: in summer, they were usually left outside when it didn't rain. Paula pushed open the door to the garage, an old out-house that could contain three cars but which usually remained unoccupied. As expected, Martine's 308 wasn't there. Unless it snowed or there was a storm, Martine usually found it simpler to leave it outdoors. Paula walked around the outside of the house, passing her own car parked by the front steps, and crossed the courtyard to go to her sister's living quarters.

The main door to the wing was locked. Paula opened it and went directly into the large studio on the ground floor, originally three adjoining rooms that she'd had knocked into one. At first glance, everything seemed in order – if that could ever be said of the jumbled bazaar that Martine worked in. The floor was strewn with sketches, torn boxes and old crumpled newspapers, piles of cloths and smudged papers, flasks, crushed tubes of paint covering the three trestle tables, on the walls were photos and pages of magazines pinned one on top of the other. Martine hadn't needed long to recreate her universe. A corner of the room had, however, been spared: it was furnished with three armchairs and an old sofa, a large low table and a plywood desk that Martine had unearthed God-knows-where, and which served as a bar. The overall effect was of a welcoming corner where Martine could rest and receive visitors. Paula felt a little calmer. This familiar chaos, the smell of paint that impregnated the air, was vaguely reassuring, a sign that her sister was alive and that she would soon be there.

There was a canvas on the easel, facing away. Paula turned it around cautiously: it was a collage of photos and oil paintings, still moist, a sort of montage that Martine called 'mixed media'. One of the photos in the composition was of a well-known actress. Paula glanced mechanically at the floor, recognising the star from the cover of a trashy magazine, which lay on the floor next to a torn page; a picture had been cut out from it. The shape fitted the photo glued to the canvas. Paula picked up the magazine and looked at the date. The issue had come out on the 19th August. Since she'd spoken to her sister two days after that, she wasn't any further forward.

She walked up the spiral staircase that led to the master bedroom, a spacious room that looked out onto the courtyard from two tall windows, and had an en-suite bathroom that was nearly as large. The bedroom was furnished with various pieces that Martine had gathered from the attic and other rooms of the house. A curious Louis XV styled chest of drawers, the veneer of which was partially unglued, supported a dozen books pressed between two cracked-porcelain bears reminiscent of François Pompon's stylized animal sculptures. An armchair of the same style – a cabriolet chair covered with faded apricot velvet – was placed by the window and next to which, within arm's reach, a pile of art journals and fashion magazines was stacked up in a contemporary Plexiglas magazine rack. On top of a Napoleonic desk, a computer slept under its cover. Martine never used it ("I.T., boooring!" she always said; she never even used the internet). An antique sea-chest sat proudly at an angle, a dress gracefully draped over the half-opened lid as if it were in the shop window of briefcase store. The bed wasn't made, the bedspread had simply been rolled up onto the pillows.

Paula walked over to the wall-to-wall closet and slid open the door: the closet was full, and it looked like all of Martine's clothes were there. Her two suitcases were still on the shelf, alongside her large leather bag. She hadn't, therefore, left to go somewhere.

A visit to the bathroom confirmed this impression: on the washbasin shelf and on the dressing table, none of her toiletries seemed to be missing (two bottles hadn't even had the tops put back on). Martine's dressing gown was hung on its peg. A few bits of jewellery lay in a drawer that she hadn't bothered to close; all in all, nothing out of the ordinary.

And yet, walking back downstairs, Paula felt uneasy, something nagged at her, as if she had just walked past a hidden piece of information but hadn't been able to notice it.

Returning to the kitchen, she noted that it was five to midnight. The telephones still lay mute. Surely, something must have happened. It wasn't like Martine to let her drop without a word, or even a call.

Paula thought of Youri - the boyfriend that Martine had left three months earlier, fleeing back to Boyrive after two turbulent years living together with him, a period interspersed with fights, forgiveness, week-long break-ups and passionate reconciliations. Youri was a Yugoslav sculptor who was just becoming known. Paula told herself that Youri could very well have spontaneously invited Martine to a dinner of explanations, regrets and promises... the kind of situation where everything else must be dropped and forgotten, even if you have to telephone to apologise the next day. Maybe Martine had been convinced to go back to Paris with him. Youri knew how to make himself irresistible when he wanted, he was cheerful, funny, and incredibly generous! Whenever he sold a sculpture, he would invite up to ten people to dinner at a time, he'd give presents to the whole family, or take Martine away for romantic weekends in New York or London... the following day, he would be solemn, filled with self-doubt, despairing of his talent and his work. He would hole himself up for a week at a time in the ancient locksmiths workshop in Montrouge that he used as his studio, his only company a crate of Wyrobova vodka. Youri had two faults: alcohol and jealousy. He smothered his partners with a violent and exclusive love. All in all, he was unbearable. Never mind that Paula had always had a soft spot for him.

He was completely different to Martine's first husband, Dr Bruno Dutilleux, who had put Paula off at first glance. A young, arrogant and ambitious surgeon, a man with two faces: all honey and diplomacy in public, intolerant and authoritative at home. A handsome guy, if you will, but still a young cockerel, idolised by his mother. He expected unconditional admiration from the women of his entourage, and reared up at the slightest contradiction. He had once crushingly put Paula in her place in front of several people during dinner. And the most surprising thing wasn't that he'd insulted her – in that cutting tone, in front of everyone – it was his sudden anger, his livid expression. He didn't like Paula because of the influence she had on her younger sister, an influence that he believed prevented him from moulding his young bride as he would have wished. He didn't like Martine's first attempts at painting either, insidiously discouraging her. Towards the end of their relationship, he would readily slap Martine, and she finally left him. Martine had bizarre taste in men. Molly-coddled since her childhood by her parents and then her older sister, maybe she felt the need to put herself in danger.

In comparison, Paula's existence was quite stable. She had met her husband in Milan where she'd been invited to a friend's wedding; André was in Milan on business. They'd stayed at the same hotel, Via Manzoni. Sometimes, people's paths cross by chance - people who should never have met otherwise - and, without them really noticing at first, the image of the other is imprinted in their minds and won't let go. When she left in the morning, and when she would come back in the evening, Paula's eyes would sweep the hotel hall and, when she saw this man standing by the reception, or sat in an armchair at a distance watching her over the top of his newspaper (since he read Le Monde, she guessed that he was French), her heart would leap in her chest. They must have felt that they were made for each other, since Paula extended her stay a little and André told her later that he had done as much too. She waited for him to make a move. The third evening, he invited her to dinner.

Paula was twenty-two at the time, an idle, available young woman. After the death of her parents, she had failed the entrance exam to study at the prestigious École Normale Supérieure, and didn't think it worthwhile to repeat the preparatory year. What use was it to continue cramming and filling her head with things that she'd only studied to please her parents in the first place? André was ten years older than her and Director and owner of a road transport business, VasseurTransEurope, which was growing rapidly. He had built it up entirely on his own, or nearly: his father, an entrepreneur in the building trade (Jacques Vasseur SA), had helped him start up. Paula was flattered that a real man was interested in her, a man very different to her usual crowd.

"He reminds me of Robert de Niro," Martine said after Paula had introduced them to each other.

Well observed. He had that mix of manly strength and fragility, a secret sensitivity which he kept under control, whilst on the surface he had a mischievous charm. Paula was very much in love, and they married six months later. The honeymoon period over, however, their relationship crumbled within the space of two or three years. André travelled a lot, but that wasn't really the problem as he only ever travelled for short periods. The problem was that there wasn't a deep understanding between them anymore. He was a man who knew how to conduct himself. He was present at family events, and never forgot birthdays. He took care of life's tiresome details. He was courteous towards his wife. Paula knew he held her in high regard, and in one sense he was proud to have an independent and educated wife. When they went out together, he appreciated her elegance. And yet somehow she felt that he would have preferred a softer, more feminine wife, someone who was less sure of herself and her decisions: someone more dependent. Paula had lost the freshness of her youth, and he found her too thin, too hard. Realising that her husband didn't really love her, or in any case that he didn't love her deeply, Paula distanced herself. They didn't have children. In the beginning, they weren't in a hurry, they had agreed to wait. Subsequently, they didn't talk about it anymore - as if they knew that they wouldn't stay together.

Coming back to her thoughts, Paula continued to wait for the ring of the telephone call, the crunch of tyres on the gravel, César's barking... but the silence deepened. She shivered, tired. At half past midnight, she went to bed.

When she came down the following morning, Madame Perreira was already there. A ragout simmered on the stove, cabalhau a congregada, a Portuguese speciality: a layer of onions, a layer of potatoes, more onions, tomatoes, and large chunks of cod. She was preparing a pastry base, rolling it out on the floured work surface. Paula closed the door behind her.

"Good morning, Manuella."

"Good morning, Madame Paula."

In the enamel cafetière, the coffee was still warm. She poured herself a cup and sat at the end of the table, in spite of the smell of fish that had begun to fill the kitchen.

"Everything gone well this week?"

"Quite well. Nicholas didn't mow the lawn. Leg pain, he said."

Having been in France for thirty years, Madame Perreira had learnt to speak French almost without trace of an accent except for a soft lisp. She had lost her husband, and lived alone. Her eldest son, a mason like his father, had the travel bug and worked mostly on building sites in other countries - preferably as far away as possible. Her youngest lived in Porto where he had married the daughter of a restaurant owner. Since he'd gone to school in France and spoke fluent French, and furthermore could get by in English, he was able to welcome tourists into the restaurant with ease. "My youngest has made it," his mother would affirm with satisfaction. Indeed, as the son of a cleaning-lady and a mason, both expatriates, making his way successfully in his country of origin wasn't a done deal.

"What day did you come to work this week, Manuella?"

"Tuesday, as usual, and Thursday afternoon as we discussed."

"You saw my sister on Thursday?"

"I didn't see anyone, Madame Martine, she'd gone out."

Employed in several houses, Manuella accomplished her tasks without worrying about the comings and goings of her employers. Manuella continued:

"I just saw Madame Martine on Tuesday. I cleaned her room, but she didn't want me to disturb her downstairs. She was painting... shall I make one or two tarts?"

"Just one" said Paula.

"Monsieur André isn't coming?"

"No, he's working."

"Ah, working.... working..." sighed Manuella, without saying anything further about the thoughts that this word, obviously heavy in meaning, evoked. "Apple or apricot?"

"Whatever you want."

"It doesn't make any difference to me..."

"Apple, then. Did you see César?"

"Who?"

"My sister's dog," said Paula impatiently, "her Labrador."

"I don't know, I wasn't paying attention."

"Really!" Paula exclaimed.

"Madame, I don't remember!" protested Manuella, in a wounded tone.

Martine never went anywhere without her dog: if César was around, it was certain that his mistress wasn't far away. He was a beautiful 4 year old brown Labrador, intelligent and affectionate, a sturdy beast who made her feel safe. César was very talented: he brought her letters, knew how to open a latched door, and he sometimes found objects long thought lost. Even though he would never have hurt a fly, he would bark in a terrifying manner if he thought it necessary (for example, if he spied a wild boar in the distance during a walk in the forest , or if a stranger came to the gate). But he adored the postman and as soon as he heard the post van, which he heard before everyone else, he would run around joyfully to alert the household. He was a dog with a sense of responsibility. He loved carrying out his orders, and the moment he finished a task demanded of him, he would go and sit down next to the humans, conscious of having earned his place among them. He knew about forty words, and when he held one's gaze fixedly with those glittering chestnut-gold eyes, he distinctly gave the impression that he was going to tell you something. Paula, who would never weigh herself down with a pet, liked César a lot. He was, however, a Parisian dog, a city-dweller, not a country dog that you could leave alone for hours on end. Although he had a comfortable kennel near to the house, there was no way he was going to sleep in it. He whimpered and cried enough to break your heart whenever he was left outdoors for the night, and Martine finally laid out a blanket for him in the studio.

Methodically, trying to work out the time that her sister had disappeared, Paula went over the events in her head: it was Saturday 24th August, the cleaning-lady had seen Martine on Tuesday 20th, Wednesday 21st late morning Paula had spoken to her on the phone...

Manuella, absorbed, meticulously picked up the slices of apple and laid them out, overlapping one another, on top of the tart.

"The plumber came." She said, suddenly.

"When was that? Thursday? Did you see him?"

"No, I didn't see him. I'd told Madame Martine that the tap in your bathroom was leaking. She must have called him... Thursday, when I came back, I went to check on it and it wasn't leaking any more. He left a note to say he'd also changed the toilet flush."

She went to put the tart in the oven. "This house always needs something repairing."

Paula smiled.

"Old houses are like that, it's what makes them so charming."

Manuella set the timer.

"Three quarters of an hour," she said, "mustn't let it burn."

CHAPTER 2.

The difficult thing about owning one of the most beautiful houses in the area - an old manor farm restored sixty years ago by their grandparents - and about belonging to a well-known family in the region, is that you cannot escape gossip. Paula was born and had always lived in Paris, where no-one knows their neighbours and the only personal question people allow themselves to ask, if they absolutely have to, is the dog's name. She was terrified by the way rumours spread in the countryside, and always tried to present the most proper, glossy image possible. Martine, on the contrary, was impervious to idle chatter: "One must let the mud flow past…"

Whilst getting ready in her room, Paula wondered how she should question the plumber about her sister without starting any rumours. From what Manuella had said, he must have been in the house on Wednesday – morning or afternoon – or even Thursday morning, since

Manuella had found that the pipe had been repaired on her arrival in the afternoon. Maybe the plumber had seen Martine or noticed something? She needed to find a reason to talk to him without awakening his curiosity: maybe another pipe to repair...

Whilst waiting, she decided to call the Gendarmerie – the local branch of the police. She didn't believe that her sister had had an accident since she'd left with both her handbag and her diary. If, however, she had been hurt en route, Paula believed that the Gendarmerie would probably already have called her. But even so, she'd prefer to make sure.

Boyrive, where their house was situated, was a hamlet in the Neuville district, a large market town with four thousand inhabitants on the southern end of the Seine-et-Marne area, bordering Beauce and Gâtinais. Paula knew the Brigadier Chief a little; they usually met at the annual Mayor's gathering at the Town Hall, or at the celebrations held throughout the year that make up the rhythm of community life. He was a policeman of the Gendarmerie, in his forties, nearing retirement, pleasingly round about the waist, but known for being firm-handed beneath his debonair exterior.

He started talking immediately, without her having to wait.

"Brigadier Chief Gallard, good morning, Madame," he said amiably.

"Good morning Brigadier, how are you?"

"I'm very well, thank you. What can I do for you?"

Worried that no-one would take her seriously if she seemed panicky, Paula tried to stay calm as she explained.

"It's about my sister... we were supposed to meet up yesterday in Boyrive, but she wasn't there. You know that she's been living in the house for three months now, since the beginning of June in fact?"

"I'd been informed, yes. All alone in that big isolated house, it's not a very good idea," he observed, concerned above all with ensuring peace reigned in his district.

"Well, my sister disappeared on me and there was no message from her. She hasn't telephoned me either. I've been waiting for her in Boyrive since yesterday evening."

"It's too early to worry," the Brigadier responded, predictably.

"I'm not really worried, but she doesn't usually do things like this. We'd arranged three days ago to meet up and everything seemed fine, and we were looking forward to spending the weekend together."

The Brigadier Chief had a busy day ahead of him.

"What do you want me to do?" he asked, his tone bored yet polite.

"I want to be sure that she hasn't had an accident, that nothing has happened to her on the road."

"What does she drive?"

"A navy blue 308, registered in Paris. Her licence plate is 83 something... I don't remember the full number. It's a 308 with leather seats..."

"A 308 with leather seats" the Brigadier repeated thoughtfully, "you don't see one of those everyday"

"...light grey leather seats."

"The last time you saw your sister was in Boyrive?"

"I didn't see her, I was still in Paris. We talked on the phone. It was Wednesday around eleven-thirty, midday."

"She was at home?"

"Yes, definitely, I called the landline."

"I haven't heard anything about a 308," said the Brigadier. "If she'd had an accident, you would have heard about it."

"Yes, of course, no doubt about it. I'm sorry for disturbing you." Paula stopped speaking, and waited. The Brigadier suddenly realised that he was expected to say something.

"I'll look into it," he said "it's premature, but I'll see what I can find. You're staying in the vicinity?"

"I'm not moving."

"I'll ask around and I'll let you know."

When she'd hung up, Paula thought of the hospitals. Putting the question of a possible car accident to one side, Martine could have fainted, or had a seizure. At that very moment she could be ill or alone somewhere... Under the age of thirty, people believe they're invincible, and then there's a tennis match that's a bit too aggressive, a long jog under the hot sun or even for no apparent reason, you're suddenly gone: severe hypoglycaemia, cardiovascular disease, cardiac arrest...

Sudden amnesia? In the cinema you see films of people who suddenly don't know who they are any more, who wander aimlessly in the streets until a kind soul takes them to the hospital. Overworked as the hospitals are, perhaps they haven't yet had time to call her family. Paula thought sadly, "I'm her family, her only family."

Then she thought of the drugs. Martine occasionally took cocaine: she claimed that it helped her work, that it stimulated her painting. This habit was a gift from her ex-husband. Bruno Dutilleux had friends in show-biz, and he loved strutting about with celebrities. When they were married, throughout the year he and Martine were invited to cocktail parties, premieres, opening events at nightclubs or new restaurants. Paula went with them once, when André was away travelling. It was the official opening of a gigantic nightclub in

Neuilly, which belonged to the singer and crooner Serge Savil, who was, according to the newspapers, a sort of French Sinatra who had sold millions of records during a career that spanned twenty years. When they arrived, an insane crowd jostled impatiently in the street, shouting and brandishing invitation cards without even being able to get inside, it was already so full. They had only been able to get in themselves thanks to Bruno's mate, a retired champion swimmer turned film actor (Paula thought his acting was mediocre). They found themselves with ten other people in the VIP section, around an immense low table, on velvet seats so large and deep that they could almost have slept there. Standing near them, the groupies danced (or rather, wiggled), on the spot, half-nude in glittery scraps of cloth that were supposed to pass for dresses. Soon enough, their companions started to journey between the table and the toilets, where they discreetly snorted lines. Later, drugs were openly circulated: Prozac, ecstasy, and all sorts of new products that Paula had never heard of – so various and so easy to obtain that they could have been listed in the menu, slotted between the champagne and the whisky. It was around this time that Martine started taking coke. Even though her consumption had diminished significantly since her divorce, she still took some from time to time, despite the remonstrations of her sister.

"That club is a cover up," André remarked when Paula told him about her evening, "it's there for money laundering."

"Oh? How do you know?"

"I just know, that's all. Savil is crippled with debt. He's helping someone out."

Bruno returned the favour by inviting his trendy set of friends to Boyrive. It was painful to see them on summer weekends, slumped in the deckchairs around the swimming pool, overwhelmed with tiredness and boredom, a real Sempé cartoon! The star and the band: collaborators, friends, scroungers, topless girls – the girls, who followed them everywhere, distracted them for a week or two (Paula never saw the same one twice), while they rewarded them with Vuitton bags or a Versace dress, a trip to Saint-Tropez, a small part in a film for the luckiest... did they also teach them to take drugs?

In any case, it hadn't been long before they'd brought them to Boyrive. Paula was hurt, maddened: they think my house is a nightclub, she told herself, my mother's house, my grandmother's house! She never dared speak out, as they would only have been thrown out the door (and, after all, it was also Martine's home, she could invite over who she wanted), but she was worried: with all this muck and alcohol flowing liberally, she was always afraid that something would happen. When Martine got divorced, Bruno left and took his friends with him. It was a huge relief.

Paula dialled the number of the hospital in Fontainebleau.

"I would like to speak to Madame Martine Jensen, please."

"... Jensen," repeated the receptionist, looking through the database, "I can't see her here... when did she come in?"

"One or two days ago, maybe three. I'm not sure that she's actually there," she improvised, "I know she's been hospitalised but I wasn't told where."

"Hmmmm no, I can't see her listed, she's not here. You should try the Marc Jacquet hospital, in Melun – I'll give you their number."

"Thank you" said Paula.

At the Marc Jacquet hospital, a man answered the phone. He also tried his best to help her, but without success. Finally, he advised her to try the clinics, but there were three in Melun and Paula let it drop. If her sister had been hospitalised, there was nothing to say that it had been in this region. Officially, she was a Paris resident, and Paula couldn't call all the Parisian hospitals. She decided to leave the matter with the gendarmes.

It was already three in the afternoon, and she still hadn't eaten anything. She went down to the kitchen: Manuella had stepped out for a moment and the cabalhau and the apple tart lay on the stove. Paula made herself some tea and cut a slice of the tart. The scent of the cinnamon that filled her nostrils made her think of her husband: he loved apple and cinnamon. She almost thought of calling him – but what for? He would tell her what the Brigadier Chief had said: too early to worry yet.

André had stayed in Paris to work. He would have spent the whole of Saturday with his accountant at head office, on the Balzac road, near the famous Champs-Elysées Avenue. They would have been examining the figures from the previous quarter, establishing the projections for the upcoming quarter, all things that Paula only had the faintest idea of. André didn't talk to her about his business. In the beginning, she'd tried to show some interest in his work, being young enough and in love enough to believe that she should share everything with him. In the evening, she would interrogate him about his day, trying to get him to explain what his work was all about. "Nothing to get excited about", he usually responded to her questions, "transport of goods." She couldn't get anything further out of him and vexed, she finally told herself "well, there we go" and stopped asking him anything further.

She never bothered him at work, and furthermore it wasn't usually necessary: André, naturally courteous and conscious of keeping the peace at home, never forgot to warn her if he was going to be late or had to have dinner with a client. Whenever he travelled, he would call her punctually the evening he arrived at the hotel, and also the day before he came back to Paris. Paula only called him at work when it was absolutely necessary and any communication was always brief: from a sense of discretion, without doubt, a sort of pride. But above all, because she didn't get on with the phone. Hers nearly always went straight to the messaging service, which she would listen to once a day with boredom. When her friends managed to get hold of her, she would usually interrupt their chatter with an invitation to meet up for a drink, or to accompany her somewhere. And she'd stopped using her mobile a long time ago. Irritated by other people's ringtones, she was even more disturbed by her own which made her jump and then rummage frantically through her bag – ringing all the while – under the impatient gaze of those around her. She didn't like being called whilst walking down the street and having to walk in a ridiculous manner, her hand glued to her ear, as if she'd had a sudden attack of earache. Out of habit, and because they were the only numbers in her address book, she preferred to call landlines.

She looked out of the window. It was a beautiful day: a golden end-of-summer afternoon, a little muggy. Not a leaf was moving. Paula hadn't stepped outside since getting up, and decided to go out and take her mind off things. Her tea was getting cold: she emptied her cup and forced herself to finish her slice of tart without much gusto. On swallowing the last mouthful, however, she changed her mind: she went back to the telephone and called her husband. The phone rang five or six times without any reply. Leaning on the support stand, Paula glanced at the clock: three thirty. She dialled the number once again. For a long time she listened as it rang and rang, calling into the emptiness.

The moment she hung up, she heard a knock at the window: the plumber was smiling at her through the glass. Happy to see him (and she wouldn't have to find an excuse to contact him now), she motioned for him to come in.

"Good afternoon Monsieur Morel", she said, shaking his hand, "how are you?"

"I'm well, Madame Jensen, struggling on." (Even though she was married, the people of Neuville who had known her parents continued to call her by her maiden name.)

"It's a lovely day today, isn't it? A real pleasure to go out when it's like this," said Paula, knowing very well that in the countryside it's not considered polite to broach the real subject of conversation immediately.

"Yeeees, but it won't last. Gonna be a storm soon."

"How is your family? Your children? Your little one is going back to school soon, isn't she?"

"Everyone's fine, Madame Jensen, thanks. My little Jocelyne is going to primary school this year. That'll help Madame Morel."

"Oh, I can imagine," said Paula, "four children must be a lot of work for her," she said, her large, open eyes looked at him questioningly.

"I came back to change a part," the plumber responded to her mute interrogation, "I didn't 'ave everything I needed in my van, I just put in a temporary washer. It won't take more 'n ten minutes. Didn't know there'd be anyone 'ere so I got the keys from Nicholas when I went by."

Nicholas, the gardener, lived a hundred meters from the house. As well as doing the gardening, he was also a kind of caretaker, and from time to time would do an inspection round of the house.

"Does he still have a bad leg?" asked Paula.

"It's his sciatica playin' up again."

"It's very painful, the sciatic nerve. I'll go and see him a little later."

"With your permission, I'll go up," the plumber said, pulling his bag strap onto his shoulder, "I don't 'ave very long."

The plumber was a regular in the area. A good workman, competent and clever, he wasn't the type to tell you to replace the whole system when you'd only called him for a leaky tap. The old pipe installations gave him regular work, and his customer base extended as far as Fontainebleau. Even if they could afford it, people balked at gutting their houses, especially those most in need of restoration with their miles of pipework. But then, as Morel would always say, the old pipe systems are often sturdier than the new ones.

"It's done," he announced as he came down, "that should 'old for a while."

Paula opened the dresser door.

"Of course, you'll have a drink before you go?"

"It's really a little early for that" he said, putting down his bag even so.

"A beer, a tote of whisky?"

"Well, maybe just a small beer"

She put two glasses on the table and took the tops off two bottles of beer.

"My sister called you about the bathroom?" she said whilst pouring the beer.

"Yes, it was Madame Martine. She called Tuesday afternoon."

"When did you come?"

"As soon as I could… the next day, Wednesday. In the afternoon, actually. I had things to do in the mornin'. Cheers, to your 'ealth!" he said, lifting his glass.

"And here's to your health, Monsieur Morel," said Paula, doing the same, "there wasn't anything special to take care of in my sister's part of the house?"

"She didn't ask me – I didn't see Madame Martine, actually, she'd left the door open so I didn't need to disturb 'er. Especially since she 'ad a visitor." The plumber continued "There was a Ferrari by the door."

"A Ferrari..." repeated Paula, stupefied.

"Yep, a red Ferrari with black leather bucket seats, and a dashboard – should've seen it – a dashboard like an airplane! And tyres big as that - " he said, spreading his hands fifty centimetres, "now that's a car that is, you can take a bend at a 'undred and twenty miles an hour without coming off the road with an engine like that..."

"The speed limit's seventy," Paula replied mechanically.

"... precision mechanics, should 'ear the motor roar!" continued the plumber, not letting this mundane remark put him off, "A real gem! Ah, it's gorgeous but it needs a lot of care, it only starts when it has a mind to, 'ey, it's a lot of bother."

Paula looked at him; in his threadbare, stained jacket and jeans, his misshapen baseball cap stuck on his head, and the dilapidated van waiting outside for him - more like a mobile hardware store where he put his whole mess of a box of tools and spare parts - talking about this luxurious Italian car as though it were a familiar object with which he could feel some sort of affinity.

"You seem to know a lot about Ferraris," she said, as seriously as she could.

"My brother-in-law works in a garage."

Paula swallowed a mouthful of beer, guessing he'd had a close look at the car.

"The Ferrari wasn't registered in France, though?"

"Yes, it was, in Paris! Gotta be minted to be able to afford that. Even second-hand, it could fetch anything in the 'undreds of millions of francs... it's not a car for everyone."

He finished his glass with a swig.

"Thanks, Madame Jensen. Better go, now. I've another client to see. 'Ave a lovely weekend."

"And you, have a nice weekend Monsieur Morel," said Paula, opening the door for him. "Send me the bill - in euros, mind!"

"Understood, Madame Jensen, I'll do that. Goodbye, Madame Jensen, 'til next time."

Paula went upstairs scolding herself. For nearly twenty-four hours, she'd been worried to death, when Martine had simply been swept off her feet by a playboy! At that very moment, she was probably sunbathing on a beach in Cannes or Marbella. She'd gone without luggage, which of course meant that it must have been a spontaneous decision! Her friend must have taken her out to dinner. After a few glasses of good wine, with the Ferrari at the doorway ready to go, the desire to get away from it all - taking nothing with them - took hold... A Ferrari is, in itself, an invitation to fly away.

She'd done it herself once with André (although in a rather less flamboyant car): they were having dinner at a country inn one summer's evening and, instead of going home, in the blink of an eye they were at Deauville for the weekend, and bought everything they needed right there. It's certainly what Martine must have done. She'd either taken César with her or left him in someone's care (maybe with Nicholas, she only had to go and see). Paula vigorously brushed her hair and slipped on her chinos: after all this emotion, it would do her good to get some fresh air. "Just think," she mused, "I even alerted the Gendarmerie!" She then thought of the missing 308... but if her sister's car wasn't there, it's simply because she must have left it at the garage for a service or some repair. No point in worrying. Martine had decided to escape for a few days. On Monday, once she had awoken from her dream-world, she would phone.

Paula walked with small strides towards the gardener's house. She found him sat in front of the door, in the middle of sharpening the hedge-trimmer. Although he wasn't young anymore, being seventy years old at least, he was a terse and robust man who'd spent his whole life working outdoors, despite the sciatica that immobilised him for periods at a time.

"How are you, Nicholas?" she said, entering the courtyard, "I heard you were ill. Is your leg still bothering you?"

She knew immediately that César wasn't there; otherwise, he would have recognised her straight away and would have thrown himself on her with joyful barking.

"It's getting better, it's calmed down. I'll be ready to get down to work next week."

"It's not urgent. Relax a bit, make the most of the nice weather. What a lovely summer's end, isn't it?"

"Oh yes," Nicholas responded tersely, as though he couldn't care less. He wasn't a chatty man, being used to solitude. He talked more eagerly to his plants than to people.

And no hello, no smile, Paula noted. He hasn't even stopped his handywork to talk to me, pig-headed as he is.

"Tell me, Nicholas, I'm popping over to Neuville. Do you need anything?"

"Not to worry, I'm fine. My son came by earlier, he brought me everything I need."

"Alright, I'm off then. Look after yourself" she called out, passing the gate and setting off down the path.

"That's it, run off, my beauty" murmured the gardener to himself, examining the edge of his hedge-trimmer.

By the back-roads, Neuville is two miles from Boyrive, but it's also possible to get there by cutting through a forest path inaccessible to cars, which made for a lovely walk of just over a mile. Paula set off: she loved this shortcut. At the end of the afternoon, when the sun cut through the foliage in slanting beams, the forest took on an unreal aspect. As a little girl, during holidays spent at her grandparents', she often came here to take a walk: the place reminded her of picture books that, when opened, raised up pop-up cut-outs of chateaux, then trees and thatched cottages in successive layers to give the impression of depth. Though past thirty, she still saw this place through a child's eyes. When she ran, an optical effect created by her own movement and the vibrations of the light gave the impression that the branches moved, drawing aside so that she could pass. Sometimes, she caught sight of the surprised head of a doe between the bushes, or a daring young rabbit darting in front of her like an arrow. So close to Paris, this fairy-tale forest.

She covered the distance to Neuville by alternating a quick march with small strides, and arrived at the village without even getting out of breath.

While Neuville is accessible by a national road, it is fortunate in being spared from the floods of lorries which are obliged to take another route. The only traffic, therefore, consists of personal vehicles. As for those coming from abroad, most are tourists from the north heading to the middle of France: Germans, Belgians, English, Dutch - some of whom stop overnight at the Hotel de la Poste to have a break and a good meal. Opposite the train station, Neuville had a roadside café where railway workers and truck drivers stopped when they had to spend the night either at the depot or on the bunk in their vans. Around the village's main square, Martroi Place, two other cafés faced each other. One had a large newsagent's shop and lottery counter, packed with gamblers on weekends and market days; the other was The Old Oak, so called because of the two-hundred-year-old tree that decorated the central strip of Martroi Place, but which regulars simply called 'Yvette's' after the name of the landlady. It was a spacious café, but one that Yvette had also been able to keep warm and inviting by furnishing with antique benches, old lamps, solid burnished wood tables, and, at the back of the room, a long farm table covered with a waxed cloth around which thirty guests could sit at a time, elbow-to-elbow. During the hunting season, the landlady would serve up rabbit stews from her own unique recipes.

Paula never came to Boyrive without saying hello to Yvette. Having bought the local newspaper and two magazines at the newsagent's in anticipation of a second night alone, she pushed open the door to The Old Oak. A dense crowd had gathered around the counter in a fog of smoke and aniseed fumes. Nothing but men, talking loudly, occasionally bursting into virile laughter and noisily clinking glasses and an infernal racket punctuated by the tinkling and the jingles of a pinball machine. The women, who never said no to a drink at the end of the week, were also sat in the room where they contributed to the background din of Saturday night revels. The Neuville Times Square, is what Martine jokingly called it.

Three young women chatted, seated around a pedestal table.

"Hey, look, she's back," said one on seeing Paula come in.

The two others tilted their chins and all three looked at her for a few moments in silence, as if to penetrate this image of a woman so different to the rest of them and who, despite the long history of her family in the region, seemed so out of place.

"But did y'see what she's wearing? She's got a Chanel jacket."

With a glance at once disapproving and envious, they contemplated the two interlacing C's sewn onto the back of her jacket.

"She doesn't fancy herself at all, doesn't she?"

One girl's parents also lived in Boyrive.

"We used to play together during the holidays when we were little," she said, "and now she barely says hello to me, she doesn't know me no more."

"Well there you go, we're not good enough for her."

"And her sister, you've seen her sister Martine? Seems she lives here now, she hasn't moved the whole summer."

"What the hell does she do there?"

"Paintings. She donated one for the tombola on Bastille Day. It's a bit like Picasso, with stuff stuck on top, a whole hodgepodge, a real horror. Fortunately, I didn't win it, I wouldn't have wanted something like that in my house!"

"And what a life, that one! The elder, she's married, just about holding on. But the youngest, she's on at least her fourth by now!"

"And there you go, she's alone."

Opinion was divided in the village about the Jensen girls. Yvette, the owner of The Old Oak, for example, was sympathetic towards Paula. She thought that the sisters hadn't had much luck. To lose your grandparents just a few months apart from each other - who hadn't been as old as all that - and then a few years later to lose your parents in one fell swoop! It pained Yvette to see them so young, alone and unsupported. Their paternal grandparents didn't care for them. They lived in Copenhagen and their granddaughters had only seen them three times their whole lives. Of course, since it was their son after all, after the plane crash they came down for the funeral services (a mass in Paris, in Saint-François-Xavier, and one in the church in Neuville, since there were no bodies to bury), but they went back home soon after. The girls were grown-up, free from want: their grandparents must have thought that the girls would be able to get by... which they had done, of course, but Yvette thought they were brave, especially the eldest who'd taken on the weight of responsibility all on her own.

"Hello Madame Paula," she shouted when she saw her, to carry over the surrounding din, and she pointed towards the other end of the counter, "come over here," (signalling 'let her past' to two young men, who quietly let her through). "So, you've come to see us for the weekend?"

"Yes," Paula said, "hello Yvette, Paris is starting to fill up again now it's the end of summer, so I thought it'd do me good to have some fresh air." She looked around her, "there's a crowd this evening!"

"Like every Saturday. Can I get you anything?"

"A Ricard, please."

"It's the Goat-Farm Fete today and tomorrow," said Yvette, putting down the Ricard and a jug of water on the counter. "I went to have a look earlier, the atmosphere was electric! As well as all the cheeses, they were selling sausage and chips with draught beer, would you know!" She laughed, "They're going to be competing with me very soon up there, thank goodness it's only once a year!"

Compared with Paris, or any other big town, the lives of rural community residents could seem drab and monotonous. How wrong. In addition to the traditional festivals, faithfully celebrated, the revelry continued throughout the year in Neuville: the lunches or dinners of the Hunting Society, the Philatelic Association, the

Neuville Walkers, country meals and balls organised by the village council in their function rooms, national holidays, the Lotto, card-game contests... and even during winter nights, when the village is plunged into darkness and all is quiet and the shutters are closed, all of a sudden when turning a corner there are the bright lights from the windows of a room full-to-bursting, in front of which dozens of cars are parked, and where the residents of Neuville are in the middle of celebrating. As for concern with protocol, love rivalries, mockery and gossip, Neuville's residents have nothing to be jealous of even the swankiest of Parisian salons.

"It's never boring here!" said Paula.

"What were you expecting... we do what we can!"

Paula wanted to ask her if she'd seen her sister, but The Old Oak was the last place to ask questions if you wanted to avoid rumours. She contented herself with letting Yvette talk, hoping that she'd naturally allude to her sister, but, no.

Leaving the café, she bought a freshly-baked baguette and took the path back to the house, this time without running.

A light blinked on the telephone messaging service. Brigadier Chief Gallard was happy to inform her that no accidents involving her sister's car, licence plate 8364-BGR-75, had been recorded on French territory during the last week. It was nice to hear, even if Paula didn't really think any more that there had been a car accident.

The next day, having slept badly and determined to go back to Paris, her husband called while she was packing her bags.

"Everything ok?" His voice was relaxed.

"Yes," said Paula, "but I'm coming back. I've been alone since Friday, Martine isn't here."

"Why's that? Didn't you arrange to meet?"

"Yes, we did. I don't understand it. She must have left to go somewhere, I'll explain it all later."

"She didn't leave you a note? She didn't telephone?"

"Well, no…"

"You seem tired, my dear, you're worried…"

"A little. I called your office yesterday to talk to you about it but no-one was there."

"What time?" asked André, a little too quickly.

"About half three."

"We were on Berri Street," he replied, also a little quickly, "we'd gone to get something to eat. Don't worry too much about Martine, my darling, you know her. You'll be back at the house for lunch?"

"Yes, not much traffic on Sunday mornings."

Before leaving, she went back to her sister's apartment. She still had that nagging feeling that the rooms contained clues that she hadn't been able to pick up on. Entering the bedroom for the second time, she immediately understood: relatively speaking, Martine's place was too tidy. Even if the bed hadn't been made and was only covered by a bedspread, the room wasn't its usual shambles. Nearly all the clothes were hung up on the rack, jumpers and lingerie were neatly folded on the shelves and in the drawers. Instead of lying spread out on the ground, the newspapers and magazines were piled up in the magazine rack. In the bathroom, Paula could see that only one bath-towel had been used – it was rolled up into a ball under the washbasin. More importantly, the bin was nearly empty, as if it had only been used once. Everything gave the impression of having been cleaned only the previous day. Manuella cleaned at Martine's on Tuesdays. Paula deduced that her sister had therefore taken off on Wednesday evening – which would confirm the hypothesis that she'd driven off with the Ferrari owner.

Back in Paris, she felt better. In the comfort of her apartment, with her husband close by, things seemed less dramatic than in the solitude of Boyrive. Through the windows, the leafy trees of the Jacques-Bainville square, the roofs of the grand buildings on the Boulevard Saint-Germain silhouetted against the clear sky, and the murmur of cars - still faint on this end-of-August Sunday, created a reassuring, familiar environment.

André was attentive and kind. He liked Martine and knew her well since, at the beginning of his marriage to Paula, the three of them had lived together for a while on Saint-Dominique road. At that time, Paula was living with her sister in the apartment that they'd inherited from their parents. Of course, after they had fallen in love in Milan, André spent more and more time at hers, having dinner and occasionally staying over. As he usually got up first in the morning, he would make the two sisters breakfast, so that, when they got up after he'd left, they would find the table set and the coffee ready. When he and Paula were married, he only had to bring over his bags. The apartment was big enough for three people to live in comfortably without bothering each other, or even seeing each other on days when they just wanted to be alone. This temporary situation was endlessly extended for the simple reason that they were comfortable as they were. André didn't mind being mollycoddled by the two women, and he loved taking them both out to dinner, making a grand entrance in restaurants flanked on either side by these two stunning blondes. It was an amiable cohabitation, and one probably spiced with pleasant musings. It was a period of grace, as occasionally appear in everyone's lives, a few years or a few months of dancing above it all, feeling insolently strong, believing it will never end... and then, with time, this happiness that one thought was invincible crumbles, and we find ourselves once again fragile, anxious in fits and starts, half-unhappy like most people.

Martine had gotten married and went to live with her husband, the dashing Dr Dutilleux. Barely three years later, she was back with them (she went back to her sister's place like others go back to their mother's). They lived together for a while longer (what André called the Second Cohabitation) but it wasn't the same anymore. The spell was broken. The insouciance, that feeling of invulnerability, had disappeared. Martine seemed morose, as though a light had gone out in her: she took two rooms at the back of the apartment and threw herself into her painting, only coming out when necessary.

And one year later, Martine met her sculptor, Youri, and went to live with him on the Boulevard Montparnasse. She'd left them the apartment and things carried on like that. André gracefully thanked her each year with a get-away trip, or by renting a chalet in the mountains for her, or by buying her some jewellery that Paula helped him choose.

Having given her husband an account of the weekend's events, Paula spent the afternoon sorting out the post: paying bills, saying 'yes' to invitations that she didn't really want to accept, writing to say congratulations or send condolences – an activity which enabled her to both catch up on correspondence and keep her occupied.

That evening, André took her out to dinner in a nearby restaurant, a great Italian that welcomed a number of Ministry employees for lunch, as there were lots of Ministry buildings in the area, and in the evening received local residents who liked to be able to just walk on down.

The Manager came over to say hello and take their order.

"Valpolicella?" André suggested to his wife.

"If you want."

The waiter brought the wine, and presented it to André to taste.

"That's fine."

He poured Paula half a glass, which she eyed without touching.

"Drink," André said, "it'll help you relax."

She obeyed. A soft warmth quickly spread over her, a feeling of well-being. The Valpolicella was their own personal ritual, as it was the wine they'd had in Milan during that first dinner together.

"Ariane de Frémonval's here tonight," Paula said, having scanned the room.

"Who?"

"A model, the muse of some designer."

"She's got the name of a 1900's hussy. Is she really called that?"

Paula smiled and shrugged her shoulders. She scrutinized the model's outfit, her flowing suit perfectly cut, her peach satin blouse with the little collar rising up, the two strings of pearls nonchalantly crossing on top.

"Look discretely to your right, two tables over."

"Oh yes," said André, having glanced over (he didn't like sophisticated women, he preferred, a hundred times over, a beautiful girl in jeans and a t-shirt). "She's skinny and has the neck of a giraffe," he said teasingly.

Then, noticing that Paula was picking at her salad,

"Eat, you're eating nothing. You should have ordered some pasta - in Italy they start with 'la pasta'."

He devoured his seafood tagliatelle, after which he was brought his scaloppini alla parmigiana. It would have taken a lot to make him worry. Having just reached his forties, he was still handsome, sturdy as you like, with a lightly tanned complexion, his skin glowing since he spent a lot of time outside with his vans in the business warehouses situated in La Garenne-Colombes. He drank little and didn't smoke, except for the occasional small cigar. When he was stressed, he went to the leisure centre to exercise: "He who rules himself, rules others," he'd declared to Paula one day, who'd laughed heartily – it was too pompous, not like him at all... he must have heard it somewhere.

"She's still beautiful, a really elegant woman," she said, poking a salad leaf with the end of her fork, "she's got class, that Ariane de Frémonval."

"Displaying obvious signs of her social milieu, with expensive clothes and the whole paraphernalia, is everything but elegant," announced André in a firm tone that left no room for further comment.

"Staying slim, being well-dressed for every occasion, that takes taste and discipline, it says a lot about a person," his wife replied emphatically.

"Discipline... women who work whilst also raising their children alone, now they know what discipline means."

Paula didn't reply. Even at the best of times, they found themselves more and more often on the verge of fighting. Even over nothing. But these nothings indicated profound differences in their ways of thinking. Paula had nearly gone to the prestigious École Normale Supérieure, she spoke four languages, her parents had ensured she'd received lessons in skiing, tennis, and horse-riding. Without really showing it, André disliked her sense of social superiority which, inculcated in her since childhood, seemed firmly lodged. In turn she accused him of being, in secret, a sycophant. Resentment had wedged between them. For the eight years that they'd been married, they never went as far as confronting each other: they knew where and when to stop. But in conversation, there were more and more subjects to avoid.

"How's your work going?" asked Paula.

"It's ok."

"Projections are good?"

For a fraction of a second, André looked at her, eyes wide.

"You told me that you were preparing a provisional forecast with your accountant yesterday?"

André caught up with himself quickly.

"I didn't remember having talked to you about it. Yes, the next few months should be good. It's going better since I bought new vans."

They ate for a moment in silence. Although she'd gone out with her husband to take her mind off things, she couldn't stop thinking about her sister.

"I don't want to make a mountain out of a molehill," she said suddenly, "but don't you think it's strange that Martine left like that without saying anything?"

"Yes and no. She's been alone for three months. She must have a private life."

"But to go off without telling me, without leaving a note..."

He joked, "It's the Ferrari that made her head spin!"

"A Ferrari," said Paula, "makes you think... you know anyone with that kind of car?"

"No." He thought for a moment, "It could be someone her ex-husband knew."

"But she broke off from that group a long time ago!"

"What do we know about it? She doesn't tell us everything. If I were you, I'd wait a day or two and I'd call Bruno."

"He never liked me. He'll be thrilled that I'm worried."

"He'll tell you, all the same. She's his ex-wife. If he knows anyone with a Ferrari, he'll tell you."

"Maybe she'll call me tomorrow," sighed Paula, "Or send me a telegram, I don't know."

"Probably" said André.

Having waited in vain the whole of Monday for a sign from Martine, Paula called Bruno on Tuesday morning at eight o'clock. He picked up on the second ring with a dry and professional 'Yes?' He must have thought that it was the hospital calling. Paula knew that he worked in hand-surgery; his name had been cited recently in the newspapers concerning a daring operation attempted by the team that he belonged to. She hadn't spoken to him for at least three years. He was approaching forty at present, he must have gained weight, settled down.

"It's Paula Vasseur here – Paula Jensen," she corrected herself, realising that he would remember her maiden name more easily, "Hello Bruno, how are you?"

He quickly adopted a social, slightly mocking tone. He still had that ability to instantly change his voice and attitude, which betrayed a constant concern about the effect he was producing on other people.

"My dear sister-in-law - or dear ex-sister-in-law… I'm well. To what do I owe the pleasure?"

Paula got straight to the point.

"It's about Martine. I haven't heard anything from her for a week. I wondered if you had any idea about where she might be."

"No, of course not. What do you think - "

The previous day, while she waited without leaving the house, Paula had had a lot of time to reflect on what she would say. She decided to use the half-lie that she'd prepared.

"Listen, Bruno, I'm really worried. The last time my sister was seen, she was going through Neuville in a red Ferrari. And I don't need to tell you that she didn't go unseen... Several people told me that she was with someone, that there were two people in the car." Shamelessly, she flattered Bruno, "so I told myself that with your connections, the huge number of people that you know, you'd maybe know someone who..."

He thought for a second.

"The only one of my friends who, to my knowledge, owns a Ferrari right now, is Sammy. He's bought himself a 360 Spider which he showed me a month ago, he's not just a little bit proud of it!"

Sammy Moore was a rock singer originally from Grenoble, as if his name didn't reveal as much... Paula had met him two or three times in Boyrive. He was gorgeous, about thirty, and a little crazy.

"Oh right," Paula exclaimed, sincerely surprised, "that would mean they're seeing each other?"

"Apparently," said Bruno with a little laugh.

She hesitated, "...and what about you, have you seen Martine recently?"

"My dear, since you want to know everything, Martine called me at the beginning of July. She was bored. You have to recognise that Boyrive isn't great for things to do."

"She was only living there temporarily," replied Paula, vexed, "for her work."

"Her work?"

"Her painting."

"Oh yes, her painting. Well, I took her away with me the following weekend to Deauville – in good faith, and with good intentions! I'd been invited to a friend's villa."

There was a deafening silence at the other end of the line.

"Paula, be assured, they were good people, it was a very sporty weekend. The following week, she came with me to the opening of 'Montaigne', François Duchemain's restaurant, he's the television presenter, and... well, then I saw her by chance at 'Cab' and 'Milliardaire', and another time at 'Montana'." He smugly rattled off the names of the nightclubs, not displeased to let Paula know that her sister, of her own free will, had linked up again with her old set and was once again going to places that Paula hated.

"Martine always has a lot of success, you know?"

"She didn't tell me about it."

He let out a little laugh.

"She's not a little girl any more. Maybe she doesn't tell her big sister everything."

"We were supposed to meet last Friday in Boyrive," Paula told him in a pained voice, "but she stood me up and I haven't heard from her since."

"That's not like her, actually," Bruno conceded, and recovered his 'overworked surgeon' tone, "listen, I have to go. I'm in theatre at nine thirty. All I can tell you is that Sammy is preparing an album due out in December. He's recording at the Ripert studios, Ponthieu road. Your best chance of finding him is there."

"Thanks Bruno," said Paula.

"You're welcome. Keep me up-to-date on any news of your sister." And he hung up.

Since she was already talking to Martine's exes, Paula waited until the middle of the afternoon and called Youri. He was a different kettle of fish altogether, and swiftly sent her packing. No, he hadn't seen her sister, had no desire to see her and would never see her again! He was in his studio, he was trying to work, if only Paula could understand that... a sculpture that he had to deliver in 15 days to a gallery in New York, and it just wasn't coming together! For weeks, now, he'd been making a piece of shit! It was Martine's fault, the Americans' fault for putting him under pressure, the whole universe's fault! The atmosphere was electric, and Paula realised that there was vodka in the air. The very mention of the Ferrari, that she'd made quickly, in passing, without really believing that he might know the owner, only served to drive him up the wall. He was jealous, still in love. Paula tried to calm him down, and he started to wail. Giving up on having a normal conversation, she hung up.

He and Martine had had a turbulent relationship. They loved each other, but never managed to find an equilibrium. Youri's work suffered as a result, which made him even more tense. He tormented Martine over nothing: being late by twenty minutes, smiling at someone, sometimes even over something as simple as a new dress. If a man complimented her in front of him, he darkened, refused to speak for the rest of the evening, and exploded the minute they were home. Some days he would drink endlessly, accusing Martine of preventing him from working on purpose, and, leaving with a slam of the door, wouldn't come home that night, cheating on her with the first woman who came along. In the morning, Martine would arrive at Saint-Dominique road in tears. Paula would reason with her, console her. She would stay two or three days. The calm of the family apartment helped her to come to her senses: she'd decided it was finished, she was going to leave Youri for good.

And then the pain would set in: she would start to miss him. She wouldn't swallow a morsel, her face would become gaunt, her eyes bulging out of her head. "What's wrong with her, she's like a zombie…" André would ask with alarm. And then, one evening, they'd see her come out of her room, made-up and dressed up. It wouldn't take long to guess that she was going to prowl the cafés that her sculptor frequented... and it would all begin again.

This time, however, the break seemed definitive. Martine hadn't seen Youri for several weeks and appeared to be concentrating on her work. Paula said to herself that maybe Martine was still suffering from the break-up - and it was in order to have some fun that she'd taken up with her old friends again.

CHAPTER 3.

Just opposite the Ripert Studio was a café-tabac. Paula walked around the circular tables placed on the narrow, sunny pavement and sat down inside, near to the window. It was four-thirty pm. That morning, she'd tried to call Sammy Moore. She'd been told that he wasn't there but that he'd be recording that afternoon. Having thought about it, she decided that rather than calling him, she'd surprise him: she was worried that he'd refuse to see her otherwise, using his work as an excuse. If something awful had happened to Martine, and if he had something to hide, it's probably what he would do. So there she was, hesitating in front of the entrance to the studio. It was Wednesday 28th August. Exactly one week ago she'd spoken to her sister for the last time.

She paid for her drink and made her mind up to cross the road, although not before glancing over the parked cars – no red Ferrari. He must have left it in the garage; that kind of car isn't made for traffic jams.

She rang the bell, and the door opened automatically onto a dark corridor. Coming to the end of the corridor, and not knowing what floor the studio was on, she ignored the lift and took the stairs to the first floor. There, she came across a small grey door, the only one on the floor, with a small, discrete plaque hung on it: Jean Ripert Studio.

A young woman opened the door, or rather half-opened it, just enough to see her face through the gap, and welcomed her with a brief "Yes?"

"I've come to see Sammy," said Paula, without further politeness. The girl raised two perfectly arched eyebrows, totally stupefied to see her there.

"Do you have an appointment?"

"I telephoned this morning."

The girl took on a cold tone, trying to seem intimidating, "and what is it regarding?"

"Tell him I'm here," said Paula firmly, "tell him I'm Martine's sister. Paula Jensen."

The girl opened the door fully to let her in, "come in if you like. But I can't disturb him right now."

Paula entered a cramped room, a sort of vestibule where four young men, clearly at a loose end, sat on the desk or sprawled on the armchairs with their legs extended full-length, gabbing whilst they waited. Above a small padded door, a red light was illuminated.

"It's Martine's sister," the young Cerberus threw out as she rejoined them. They began talking again as if Paula wasn't there.

Then the light went green and the girl disappeared.

"You've got five minutes," she announced on her return, and, in a more friendly tone, "they're in the middle of recording, you see?"

Paula went through the padded door and stayed put, not daring to move further. Through the window of the production department, the mixers looked at her oddly from underneath their baseball caps: she was disturbing them. In the studio, quite a large room without windows and entirely lined with an acoustic covering, Sammy was finishing giving instructions to his band. That done, he walked over to Paula, his hair dishevelled, sweating and looking tired. All of a sudden she felt a little ashamed, and practically whispered to him:

"Please excuse me for interrupting like this... I must talk to you about Martine. It's important."

He blinked, groggy as a boxer, still in the music.

"Yeah sure," he said, "we're taking a break in ten minutes. I'll join you at the café opposite."

From the table where she'd returned to sit, she soon saw him cross the road. His hair was wet and combed - he must've put his head under the tap - and had changed his clothes, now wearing an immaculate white t-shirt and black jeans. He wasn't alone. One of the boys that Paula had seen in the studio accompanied him, a hefty type. For a moment Paula was afraid that they would both come over to her table, when they separated on arrival. The giant stayed at the counter, leaning on his elbows at the bar. Paula watched his large, rounded back: although he faced away, he seemed very aware of them. Artists like Sammy Moore, who support the livelihoods of a dozen people and bring in a fortune to the recording companies, are guarded like safes. Especially when they're recording an album: they're helped, surveyed, ferociously protected from anything that might trouble them.

Sammy pulled out a chair in front of Paula whilst acknowledging her with a rapid nod of the head.

"So?" he said, sitting down. He belonged to a world where time isn't lost on ritual greetings. Paula decided to bite the bullet.

"I don't know if you remember me. We met two or three times at my house in Boyrive, about four or five years ago."

It was around that time that Bruno had organised his parties. Then just a young singer, talented and troubled, Sammy wasn't yet the star that he'd become. Obviously, he didn't remember Paula, who only rarely and fleetingly mixed with them, when her brother-in-law invited her to join them.

"It's been a while," he said.

"You want something to drink?"

"I've already ordered." His look told Paula that that was enough for the preliminaries, and to get to the heart of the matter. She looked back at him fixedly.

"We haven't heard from Martine since last Wednesday," she said. "I know that you went to see her that day in Boyrive. Someone saw your car."

Apart from a fluttering of the eyelids, Sammy was like marble; he'd learnt to control himself. He responded, however, rather stupidly.

"You've opened an investigation?"

"I'm not joking. My sister has disappeared, it's serious. My husband and I are very worried. We're going to press charges."

The singer ran his hands through his hair, which had started to dry and fell messily over his forehead. At the same time, as though he were an impressionist who, with a simple gesture or movement of the head presents the public with an entirely new face in a fraction of a second, he let go of his macho air and his terseness, and took on the endearing expression of an innocent boy.

"If I can help at all, that's all I want."

"Tell me what you did with my sister last Wednesday."

"I went to Boyrive to ask her to spend the weekend with me. I wanted to take her to Mougins, to some friends'. But she didn't want to, she said she wasn't available. Maybe she went somewhere?"

"She was going to spend the weekend with me," said Paula. "We'd made arrangements for that Friday night, but I didn't see her. You're seeing Martine?"

"Occasionally."

"How long has this been going on for?"

"A few weeks. We met at the 'Liteship'. It was ages since I'd last seen her."

"At the light-ship?"

"It's a club," said Sammy with a non-committal gesture. "And then we saw each other again, we went out a few times, that was it."

"It wasn't serious?"

"It was a start. Why do you say 'wasn't'?" he asked, throwing her a lightning flash of his grey eyes (this boy never looked at you for long straight in the face).

"What did you do on Wednesday?" Paula asked him.

"We spent the afternoon together." The waiter put a coffee down in front of him. "I left at five o'clock because I had things to do in Paris. I had a meeting at seven pm at Fouquet's with a director. For a film project. I couldn't stay."

"What did you do with my sister?"

"Uuugh…" he smiled and lowered his head, feigning confusion; two dimples creased his cheeks.

Comedian, thought Paula. Whilst she could laugh at their screwing, all she really wanted to know was if her sister had taken anything.

"Was Martine ok when you left?"

"She was fine."

"What do you mean by 'fine'?"

"She was good, she was healthy."

"Tell me," Paula asked softly, "you didn't smoke anything, didn't take anything that could have made her ill, even after you left?"

"No!" protested Sammy, avoiding her gaze.

"Maybe she'd taken something before you got there?"

"I didn't notice anything." The guy at the bar started to shift in his seat, frequently turning his head in their direction.

"You had a drink together, though?" said Paula.

"We drank some wine, that's all."

"You didn't go out for a ride together in your beautiful car?"

"No, I told you, we stayed at her place. We spent the whole afternoon in her bedroom."

Obligingly, Paula motioned towards the counter with her chin, "someone's getting impatient."

"Yes, I have to get back, we're not finished."

"Here's my number," she said, holding out a calling card. "Think about it, please, try and remember anything you can, even just a small detail. Don't hesitate to phone me. And your friends, the ones waiting for you in the studio," she suddenly remembered, "they seemed to know my sister, maybe they know something?"

"They've seen Martine with me, that's all."

"Think about it," repeated Paula, "and call me."

"Yeah, yeah, of course," said Sammy, getting up. He hadn't touched his coffee. She pushed her diary and a pen in front of him.

"I don't have your details. It would stop me coming here to bother you." He scribbled a number on the paper.

"We'll stay in touch, yes?" she insisted.

Rejoining his guardian angel, Sammy must have seemed blue as his friend sent Paula a vindictive look. She watched them cross the road with a heavy step and a worried air. Naturally, the conversation she'd just had with the singer was upsetting, it would trouble him, and the album could suffer as a result. Paula, however, didn't care a bit.

She asked for the bill.

"It's already taken care of," said the waiter, "it's on Sammy's account."

Two days later, back from Milan where he usually spent a few days each month, André knew as soon as he entered the apartment that something wasn't right. "Madame's not well," the maid whispered to him in the hallway.

He found his wife crouched on the sofa, with a glass of whisky for company. Her eyes were red; she'd been crying. He sat near to her, and put his arm around her shoulders.

"What's wrong? What's happened?" Since she didn't reply, he added, "have you heard anything?"

Turning swiftly away from him, Paula spoke, her voice trembling.

"I've been alone for four days... and Martine... Martine...."

"I'm sorry, I had no choice. I've got some problems with a client. Big problems. I came back as soon as I could. I telephoned too, I called you every day. You didn't seem too bad yesterday evening..."

He tried to take her hand, which she pulled away in one swift movement. She gripped a handkerchief in her fist. Still without looking at her husband, she started to say, while hiccupping, "This afternoon... I went to the police station to tell them about my sister's disappearance... I took her photo... even if they didn't laugh they weren't far off... they told me that two thousand disappearances are registered each year, but most of the 'disappeared' turn up like bad pennies after a few days. Like bad pennies!" She cried without tears, in dry racking heaves. André had never seen his wife in such a state.

She continued, "One of them took Martine's photo to look at it more closely... he said 'A beautiful woman like that, she won't be short of opportunities to run off into the wilderness'..."

"What a cretin," André said. He pulled Paula closer to him. She turned back to him abruptly, and buried her head in his shoulder.

"There, there, I'm here now," he said. They remained silent for a moment.

A little bit calmer, Paula recovered some of her more usual poise.

"I didn't even tell them about the Ferrari, they would have laughed in my face... I demanded to see the Superintendant, but they claimed he wasn't there. Think about it, they weren't going to do anything about something so small."

"We'll see someone more competent, don't you worry."

"These people, you never know," Paula continued, who had never had to go to the police before, "just by going to see them, they make you feel guilty. They asked me where Martine's registered address was, and I said my place on Saint-Dominique road. Then when they learnt that we didn't live together, they looked at me like I was some kind of criminal. 'So,' they said, 'your sister doesn't live at her registered address?' I answered that the apartment belonged to the both of us, and they looked at me even more strangely as if they suspected me of having made her disappear myself! You think about it! ...As if they thought that I'd wiped out my own sister! After, they wanted to know if I saw her often, and I replied that it depended really... so, if I didn't see her often, they didn't understand why I was worried about a few days going by without hearing from her... and they seemed more and more suspicious. Since I started crying, finally, they told me that my sister was a grown woman and that she could go where she pleased. Well, 'grown women' can go and disappear for all they care, if there's no crime, they don't do anything to try and find them. Did you know that?"

"Yes," said André, "except for particular cases."

"There was one guy who seemed more serious than the rest, he advised me to inform the Gendarmerie in Neuville of Martine's disappearance and to wait without worrying too much."

"Maybe he's right. They must know what they're doing."

"Huh," replied Paula.

They set off together for Boyrive the next morning. Paula would have liked to go that very evening, but André needed to rest, and sleep for a few hours. Paula thought he looked off-colour, drawn and haggard. He seemed preoccupied, he who was usually so controlled, who carefully separated his personal and professional lives – for once, it was clear as day that he was in trouble.

They took Paula's 508. Both sisters drove Peugeots, a preference handed down from their father: the Jensens liked beautiful cars, though nothing flashy. André drove a BMW, series 5, quite a luxurious model with all the trimmings: because of his work, he couldn't do any less in front of his clients. That morning, he didn't want to drive. If Paula decided to stay in Boyrive after the weekend, she would take him to the Neuville train station on Monday morning and he would go back to Paris by train.

Given the difficulties his wife was facing, André didn't want to leave her alone. And he wanted to take in the Boyrive air, to see for himself if he could get wind of anything out of the ordinary. Even if he was careful not to open up to Paula, he found the way in which his sister-in-law had disappeared very strange. Martine loved and respected her older sister who, despite the small age difference, had always looked after her like a mother (Martine made fun of it sometimes, affectionately, and didn't hesitate to brush Paula off, calling her 'mother hen'). In any case, André didn't see Martine standing Paula up without leaving a message, and leaving her to torment herself. Worrying about his sister-in-law, a worry which increased as time went by, added to the very real and serious problems that his business was experiencing. André counted on these two days in Boyrive to step back and try and see things more clearly.

En route, Paula told him about her meeting with Sammy Moore. This boy, who held whole rooms of young spectators in his thrall, who, with one word, one rebellious sentence interjected in between two songs, who would make his audience cry with joy and stand wildly in adulation, their arms in their air, didn't appear all that nice to him. Good musician, certainly, and a great presence, but he seemed - all the same - like a fraud.

"I saw him on television once," Paula said "it was a repeat of one of his concerts. You should have seen him hypnotise the whole room, how he prepared the effects… he's a manipulator."

"They're all a bit like that," André said, "it's part of the job."

"But him… it was awful seeing his face blown up on the big screen: that satisfied little smile when he'd made the room go bananas, that sideways look underneath his lowered eyelids… he doesn't even look at his audience directly, except momentarily with a studied glance, when he wanted to get a reaction out of them." She stopped a second and then started again: "And yet, I can't imagine this guy hurting anyone, he's too caught up in himself - unless it was an accident. He's an artist first and foremost, you can tell he's only concerned with his music, especially when he's recording an album. Moreover, he has an alibi – the evening of his visit to Boyrive, he was at Fouquet's at seven o'clock. Those kind of people don't go unnoticed - he was probably seen by lots of people."

Comfortably seated in the passenger seat, André reflected on his wife's words. Actually, the idea that there had been an accident couldn't be put to one side. Supposing that, that afternoon, having drunk several glasses of wine, they'd swallowed or sniffed some muck or whatever, Martine could have been taken ill and lost consciousness... seeing her unconscious, her boyfriend gets scared: he splashes her with cold water, gives her a few slaps without being able to wake her. Panicked, instead of calling a doctor, he jumps in the car, abandoning his companion to her fate and runs to seek refuge in the bosom of his recording company, like the irresponsible asshole he is... Trouble for Sammy Moore is trouble for his producers: a huge financial loss, a great scandal in the offing. A young woman, victim of an overdose and left for dead in a manor farm by a famous singer, the press would go to town with the story for weeks... And, in this case, the only question to ask would be how far would the recording company go to get their prized singer out of a bad situation...

"What're you thinking about?" Paula asked him.

"I'm listening to you. Tell me, has Manuella cleaned your sister's apartment since last week?"

"No. I called her Tuesday morning to tell her not to touch her apartment. And I told her we were both coming this weekend to Boyrive."

"Well done. It's better that it stays as Martine left it." ...Imagine, thought André to himself, that, in order to keep their star from scandal, the producers were willing to stick their necks out, to take huge risks to cover for him. In the first instance, they could have advised him to go to Fouquet's as if nothing had happened, and to make sure to speak to lots of people. Sammy gave them the Boyrive address and Martine's mobile number. They call a number of times during the evening without getting any response. So they decide to act. In the middle of the night, some men come to the house. Since Martine's door didn't show any signs of breaking and entering, Sammy could have given them the key, or even if he'd left Boyrive in a panic, he could have just closed the door after him. So, these men come in, go up to the first floor and discover Martine's body, with César whining and howling next to her. Having done a quick tidy-up (wash and put away the glasses, take away the bottle of wine, the remains of the drugs and anything that's left behind), they take the body, and the dog too, as well as the 308 to make it seem as though she's just left. No-one's seen or heard them: coming from Paris, when you come off the B-road to take the winding back roads, the house is the first one in the hamlet, the nearest house is Nicholas the gardener's, which is only a hundred meters away, but on the other side, on the path to Neuville. So these guys double-lock the door behind them, and then they only have to get rid of the body, the dog, the key and the car..." André suddenly felt bad, overwhelmed by a wave of anxiety. He quickly reassured himself: it was only a theory, a possible scenario. He would have to ask Bruno what he knew about the recording company.

They reached Boyrive just before midday. Manuella was still there. Comforting smells wafted from the kitchen. André lifted the lid of the pot: two young guinea fowls were simmering away, next to a dish of mushrooms that waited to be thrown in.

"Ah," he said, "chanterelle mushrooms!"

"First of the season," said Manuella, "it's not rained much yet. Nicholas came to show me this morning. I took them as I know you like them."

"Very good idea," said André approvingly.

As well as the mushrooms, Manuella had done the shopping and prepared everything they needed for the weekend: an omelette that waited in the fridge, steeped in the aroma of chives, and that Paula only had to throw into the pan to cook for dinner, and a roasted veal for the next day. Two tarts warmed in the oven, Manuella's famous – and inevitable – tarts, which summed up her pastry baking talents.

She finished tossing the salad, lay the salad bowl on the sideboard, and set about unbuttoning her smock. She seemed pensive.

"There's fresh coffee in the cafetière" she said, and then, after hesitating a moment, "So, Madame Martine's left?"

Paula took out three mugs and put the cafetière on the table. She pointed to a chair for Manuella.

"Please, sit down for a moment. We have something important to tell you."

It was the beginning of her appeal for witnesses.

After lunch, Paula took the car and went to Yvette's. André was resting; they'd agreed to go to the gendarmerie together at the end of the afternoon. Paula knew that The Old Oak was a good place to collect information. When aware that one of the Jensen sisters had disappeared, it would be at Yvette's café that people would gather to talk about it, and, since it was a Saturday, it would leave them the whole weekend to mull it over and to remember what they might have seen, even a simple detail that wouldn't have struck them at the time. She arrived at a quarter to three, off-peak time. The waitress was serving the three clients at the counter.

All of the tables in the room were unoccupied, except one at the back where the owner was finishing her meal. Yvette was a widow, and had run the café on her own for many years. Even though she was small and rather delicate, she was a formidable woman who could run her own business very well, and knew how to command respect. Seeing Paula enter at this unusual hour, she understood that something had happened that was out of the ordinary – and motioned to her to join her at the table. She had just lit up a Gauloise cigarette, and held out her packet to Paula, who waved it away.

"So, it's true," said Yvette, "you don't have this horrible habit. I find that a little cigarette from time to time helps me relax. So, how are you?"

"Ok," said Paula, without beating around the bush, "I came to ask for your help. I hope I'm not disturbing you? Can you give me a few minutes?"

"Of course, go ahead. I've got all the time in the world."

"It's about my sister: I've heard nothing from Martine for ten days now. She stood me up and I've not the faintest idea of where she could be. It's the first time that she's done anything like this. We're very close, as you know."

Paula summarised the events for her; when she came to the Ferrari, seen by the plumber in the courtyard, Yvette couldn't stop herself from smiling.

"Maybe she's been carried off into the sunset?"

"No," said Paula, "I met her visitor, the owner of the Ferrari. He works in Paris right now. He assured me that he left Martine at five o'clock."

Suddenly serious again, Yvette stubbed out her cigarette, barely touched, in the ashtray.

"You want me to see what I can find out, right? Want me to try and see if anyone's seen anything? It's a delicate matter, but there's going to be a scandal, I warn you. And the gendarmes? You've spoken to the gendarmes?"

"I'm going there afterwards with my husband," said Paula, "but the police don't give a shit. The police, the gendarmes, no one gives a damn. As long as there's no crime, it's all the same to them if people disappear..." her voice was hoarse, she seemed on the verge of tears.

"Come on," said Yvette, putting her hand on Paula's, "calm down Madame Paula. We'll think through all of this. Let's go over it again: when did you see your sister last? What day did you say it was?"

"Wednesday last week, the 21st August, late morning. I didn't see her, I only talked to her on the telephone. I know for sure that she was at Boyrive then because I called her on the landline. We should have met at the house that Friday, on the evening of the 23rd."

Yvette had taken out her notebook, which she used to take down orders, and noted down the dates Paula had indicated. It was, above all, to reassure Paula and show her that she wasn't alone – since she didn't at all see how she was going to be able to help her.

"I arrived at the house at eleven pm," continued Paula, "and I couldn't find anyone. Martine wasn't there, neither was her dog, or her car; the house was deserted... I went to look in her studio – everything seemed normal. The door was locked, but she hadn't left any message, not even a note to say sorry, nothing. And she hasn't given any sign of life since then."

Yvette noticed that the customers at the counter were observing them. Through a sense of curiosity, quite natural in the countryside, they'd started to ask themselves what they could be talking about, the two of them. Even the waitress occasionally looked over in their direction.

"Marie!" Yvette called out to her, "bring me a coffee. You want one, Madame Paula? Two coffees. Your sister took any luggage with her?"

"No," said Paula, "I looked in the closet – her suitcases and travelling bag were there. You know that she'd been living in Boyrive for three months?"

"Of course, she came to see me from time to time. She told me that she intended to stay there for a while, to concentrate on her painting." Everyone knew, Yvette thought to herself, the whole village knew that a bold, beautiful young woman was living alone in that big, isolated barn, accompanied by a friendly and faithful dog. Yvette was forty-five years old. Though far from being a pessimist by nature, for the thirty years that she'd worked in the café she'd seen and heard a lot, and she didn't like the sound of what she was hearing. When they've drunk too much, men loosen up and, in their jokes or in their angry outbursts, a shocking brutality can emerge: the ramblings of drunks, no doubt, which they are the first to regret (if they can even remember them), when they reappear the next day, sheepish, their eyes puffy from their boozing the previous night, but which say a lot about their bitterness and rankled disappointments. A girl, who is at once beautiful, young, rich and with a good social standing, well, to a mind hazy with alcohol, in the heat of an August afternoon... what a magnificent opportunity to rid oneself of all one's frustrations! As for getting rid of the body, for someone who knows the forest...

The waitress brought the coffees.

"Everything is important. Everything counts," said Paula, when the waitress had left. "Even a detail that could seem insignificant... for example, if someone had seen Martine's 308, or even her dog. He's a four-year-old brown Labrador, very good-natured - "

"I know him," said Yvette, "a gorgeous dog."

" – or if anyone has seen Martine with anyone."

"Yes, of course. I'll take care of it," promised Yvette, stirring her coffee. She told herself that the best way of making people talk would be to publish a missing person's notice in the local paper, but didn't dare advise Paula to do this in case she alarmed her further.

"And in the garage? You went to see the garage? Your sister maybe left her car with them."

One of the two garages in Neuville was a Peugeot dealer. The Jensens had always entrusted them with their cars. If Martine had had the 308 serviced, there was every chance that it was there.

"I'll go there right now," said Paula. She got up, and held out her hand to Yvette: "I don't want to take up all your time. If you hear of anything, let me know... please... I'm counting on you. You have my contact details in Paris? You can call me anytime."

"Understood," said Yvette, "you can count on me. We'll see what we can do. Don't worry. " And she repeated, warmly shaking Paula's hand, "don't worry."

The troubles which had been overwhelming André for several weeks and which, despite his strength of character and his business experience, had prevented him from sleeping for more than three or four hours a night – meant that he looked like death. His troubles were, in reality, rooted in a series of circumstances that had occurred two years earlier. At that time, his import export business was running along without giving him too many problems. Without having even planned it, with a bit of luck in the location of his business to the West of Paris, and thanks to word-of-mouth, he had a large number of wealthy business clients in the cosmetics and luxury perfume sectors. His lorries exported their products throughout Europe. His clients also included the

70

shipping companies who subcontracted their road haulage to him. He couldn't complain, it was rolling along nicely, and the VasseurTransEurope lorries roamed the European roads throughout the year, especially since the opening of the borders. And then, suddenly, it all seized up. He had made a big mistake.

Stretched out on the bed, where he'd hoped to have a siesta but had found it impossible to close his eyes, André mentally replayed the film sequence depicting the chain of events that, without him even being aware of it (at least at first), had led him to his current impasse.

The film flashed back to replay a scene - one which might, at first, seem insignificant:

Monsieur Yves Rouleau, a respectable cosmetics manufacturer, was supplier to the major French brands, and his factory was located at La Garenne-Colombes, five hundred meters from André's warehouse. Until 1991, in parallel with his subcontracted undertakings, he personally undertook the export of ten thousand cases of lipstick to the USSR each month, by rail in the SNCF freight containers, destined for State-run shops. At the time it was a risk-free undertaking, paid in ready money using a Swiss bank as an intermediary. After the dissolution of the USSR, new markets opened up. A shrewd entrepreneur, with numerous contacts already in place, M. Rouleau prospected French retailers who were starting to gain a foothold in the large Russian towns, as well as local wholesalers. He started getting in a few orders. It wasn't long before his lipstick, rechristened 'Rouge de Paris' which came in a range of shades and was packaged in elaborate gold gilding, was a sensation: it's what the advertisers called a 'little luxury', one which even humble Russian employees could afford for themselves. Orders were renewed and, as M. Rouleau applied himself to extending his client base, they quickly and noticeably increased. Soon unable to meet all the consignments by himself, as they now numbered in the hundreds of millions each month, M. Rouleau went to André, who had been recommended to him by a colleague. They both agreed on one dispatch per month.

At first, it all went marvellously. The first two lorries of VasseurTransEurope arrived at their destination without hassle. And then his luck changed. One evening, coming out of Smolensk, while the driver was eating in a restaurant – which his colleagues thought to be okay – he was conveniently delayed by an obliging Russian, who gave him helpful advice about the country. As he prolonged his dinner, André's third lorry, parked behind the restaurant, was completely stripped of its wares. Sheepish and worried, the driver returned to La Garenne a few days ahead of schedule.

Comprehensively insured, André took the hit and his client, having reassured his buyers, hurried to charter another lorry in order to honour his orders. Fortunately, all went well. On the next journey, however, the driver was coming out of another restaurant – a roadside cafe where he had eaten without staying long, having taken care to park the lorry between two 15-tonne vehicles – and was dumbstruck as he searched in vain for his vehicle: it had been stolen along with its cargo. This time, the driver returned to France under his own steam, hitching a lift with compassionate fellow truckers, and presented himself at the warehouse on foot.

André's insurance premiums rose. He passed on the cost to his client, who, considering the splendid margins that he was taking on these red sticks and the juicy markets potentially opening up to him in the new Russia, decided to file it under 'profits and losses'. And the flood of lipstick lorries continued.

Then, however, things got complicated. These days, hold-ups are all the rage: one moonless night, a driver got kidnapped on a forest road along with the lorry and the merchandise. Left without news for several days, André and his client grew afraid. Pestered by the shop buyers and the wholesalers who were asking for their wares, M. Rouleau managed to buy a little time: completely powerless, the cosmetics manufacturer and his transporter could only wait, worried sick. Fortunately, and to everyone's general relief, the driver resurfaced, though a little the worse for wear. They welcomed him with open arms and asked what had happened. He had been attacked at three in the morning between Minsk and Smolensk. His attackers had blocked the road with their car; two of them had forced him back into the driving seat and made him drive, a revolver pressed against him (he can still feel the coolness of the barrel on his neck). Drive to where? He didn't know, into the forest, the Russian forest... It's a miracle that he was able to escape.

André realised he'd dodged a bullet. He considered the whole affair a warning: the next time, certainly, they would kill the driver. There was no longer any question of undertaking such hazardous journeys; he wasn't going to risk the lives of his drivers for lipstick. M. Rouleau, who was really just a well-meaning cosmetics manufacturer, was of the same opinion. Sick at heart, he mourned the loss of this promising market, and looked for other opportunities. Japan, maybe, or Singapore. They agreed that the whole thing could have been a lot worse; but everything considered, they had come out of it okay.

Three weeks passed, and M. Rouleau received a phone call...

Interrupting André's train of thought, the bedroom door banged open.

"You sleeping?"

"No."

Paula came in and sat down on the edge of the bed where her husband was lying, his hands crossed under his neck, eyes to the ceiling.

"I went to talk to Yvette."

"What did she tell you?"

"She's going to do what she can. You know, in the cafés, people chat away. She's a smart woman. If she's clever about it, she could glean some useful information. Well, if people talk. You saw Manuella's reaction when I tried to ask her some questions this morning: she hadn't seen anything, hadn't heard anything, impossible to get a word out of her. She nearly ran out the door when she left, you would've thought her pants were on fire. People are afraid, so there we go. They don't want to get involved in such things, because then they have to get involved with the police. "

"Above all, Manuella isn't French, she doesn't feel at home here."

"Then, I went to the garage, Martine's 308 wasn't there. In fact, the last time they'd seen the car was in mid-July for a minor service. Martine had had the lights done and the brake pads looked over, the guy at the garage looked up the date in the book. But even so, seeing the stack of newspapers in the garage gave me an idea…"

If she could actually do something, Paula felt better. There is nothing worse than passively waiting for news.

"… what about putting a missing person's notice in the papers, like the Courrier de Seine et Marne?"

"We should first of all talk to the gendarmes. We're still going at five o'clock?   We've still got an appointment?"

"Yes, but you know what I think, I'm not expecting anything to come of it. When I was coming back, I went by Nicholas' place; since he doesn't live far away, I thought maybe he'd noticed if there'd been anything odd."

"True, he's a country man, he's got a quick ear…"

" - and he's a light sleeper. Unfortunately, last week, he had an attack of sciatica, the doctor had given him a sedative. He slept like a log each night."

"And during the day?"

"Didn't see anything, didn't hear anything…like Manuella."

At the appointed time, Paula and André went to the Gendarmerie. They waited a moment in a small, austere room that smelt of bleach before being ushered into the office of Brigadier Chief Gallard. He promptly stood up to welcome them and warmly shook their hands (his cordiality, at that moment, convinced Paula that he was finally disposed to help them).

Having invited them to sit down, the Brigadier returned to his desk. His fingers crossed on his desk blotter, he turned to Paula with an understanding smile.

"So, I suppose you've come to talk to me about your sister?"

It hadn't been difficult to guess: he had, himself, investigated Martine's 308 a week earlier. Once again, Paula recounted the whole story, without forgetting Sammy Moore and his car, since the singer seemed to be the last person to have seen Martine. From the way in which the Brigadier nodded his head while he listened, with his benevolent and patient manner, she could clearly see that Martine's disappearance – which, for her, was a painful reality – was, for the Brigadier, a banal incident that he had already filed under his statistics. And he regaled them with the statistics, like the police had in Paris: two thousand disappearances each year in France, of which ninety-five percent, fortunately, pop up again after a few weeks.

Despite his desire to appear agreeable, Brigadier Chief Gallard never lost sight of the fact that his responsibility was keeping the peace in Neuville and the several surrounding villages and hamlets, and not to send his men out scouring the countryside searching for a young woman, who was reputed to be unpredictable, and who'd probably just taken off for a while. He asked,

"What is your sister's registered address?"

"Our place, in Paris."

"Well in that case, you should make enquiries in Paris."

"But she was in Boyrive when she disappeared! She'd lived here since June!"

"Nothing proves that she disappeared in Boyrive," the Brigadier calmly replied, "try to understand, Madame, your sister left with her car and her dog; it seems for all the world as though she's left of her own free will."

André intervened.

"My sister-in-law would never have gone anywhere without telling her sister, they're very close. What you have to understand is that it's the strength of their relationship that makes the whole thing very difficult to believe."

The Brigadier kept back a sigh: he was now being asked to psychoanalyse the whole affair! He, who after twenty years of marriage still didn't understand what exactly his wife wanted, and whose son – a snappy teenager who confronted him over everything – made him feel like a stranger. And now he was being asked to consider the deepest motivations, the state of mind of the people who paraded one after the other through his office to tell him their troubles, to complain about their neighbours, their friends, their parents even! It was all he could do to listen to them. He responded,

"People sometimes act in an unpredictable manner. Even towards those who know them best, you can believe me."

"You don't think that my sister could have been kidnapped and ransomed?"

"You would have already heard something. In this type of situation, the abductors have no wish to hang around. No one has contacted you?"

"No," said Paula, "but you're going to look into it, aren't you? You're not going to leave us hanging?"

"We're going to have to be patient. All we can do for the moment is wait." Seeing her distress, the Brigadier added, "you should contact the JRRIS in Paris, there's almost certainly one in your neighbourhood."

"…?"

"The Judicial Reception, Research and Investigation Service."

"What do they do? Can they do anything?"

"Maybe. At the very least, you could tell them about your sister, for example, tell them if she was depressed, they'll see if they're able to help you, to advise you."

"Martine was doing very well," Paula replied dryly, "I'd spoken to her two days previously, she was doing great."

"Go and see them," advised the Brigadier, "it's a Judiciary Police unit, they could be helpful."

"But are you going to open an investigation?" insisted Paula, nearly begging.

"Investigate what? Your sister is an adult and there's been no breach of law and order."

"We thought about publishing a missing person's notice in the local press," André put forward.

The Brigadier thought quickly of the consequences: his district in turmoil, panic in every house where there was a girl, the pressure put on the Gendarmerie… However, since he wasn't opening an enquiry, he couldn't stop them from doing so.

"I wouldn't advise it, you'll worry everyone around here, and I have no doubt it would be of no use."

"What about me," replied Paula vehemently, "I can't just stay here with my arms folded, waiting. To start with, I'll put a missing person's notice in the Courrier de Seine-et-Marne."

The Brigadier stood up.

"I cannot stop you. Try, even so, to be patient for a little longer." He accompanied them to the door. "Madame Vasseur, please don't worry yourself too much. There is every chance that your sister will reappear in a few days and that it will all just be a bad memory."

"How pig-headed!" exclaimed Paula, when they'd reached the car, "That landed on deaf ears! All he wanted was to shrug off the problem, he just kept telling us to go back to Paris. The only thing he was worried about was keeping the village peace. He won't lift a finger to help."

André began to speak, uneasy. Although he was no less pessimistic than his wife about his sister-in-law's fate (maybe he was more so, since he'd already formulated macabre theories), he felt he had to stay positive for her.

"Calm down," he told her, "maybe the Brigadier's right: we don't ever really know people at all. Even those closest to us can have days when they act unpredictably. You want me to drive?"

"No," said Paula, "it keeps me occupied."

"Look, if you want, tonight I'll take you to dinner at the Hôtel de la Poste. It'll take both our minds off things."

They drove for a moment in silence.

"You've seemed worried for a while now," said Paula suddenly, "you don't look well."

"Work problems," responded André, always reserved on the subject.

"Serious problems?"

"Not really. These things happen in business from time to time. It'll sort itself out."

Paula smiled.

"Well, I've been told!"

Radio silence. When André decides to keep schtum, well...

"Listen," she said, "don't take this the wrong way, but even if its money problems, I can help you."

"There are banks for that," murmured André, vaguely vexed, but unable to leave such a kind offer without a reply.

"I wasn't thinking about a loan, I'm saying I'd give it to you."

At that, he was touched. This sensible young woman, careful with money, who on occasion could be really stingy (he sometimes teased her about it), this bourgeois who had enough to live on comfortably – although, of course, she wasn't the richest – was offering him money! During the years that he bored himself silly at the HEC Paris Business School, he'd known rich women, overprotected by their fathers, guided by their ambitious mothers, and used to getting everything they wanted: under the veneer of good manners, they were incredibly selfish. It was at that time that he realised that women liked him. Glossy beauties, sure of themselves, whom he would never have dared approach took the initiative to invite him out for an evening or to a dinner with friends. He was flattered, but it never lasted long. He found simple girls more attractive, those who were less intimidating and who he felt might need him. In some ways, his own wife intimidated him; in his heart, he worried that he wasn't up to her standards, that he wasn't brilliant enough. And then, at the very moment that she was hurting, instead of thinking of her grief she was offering to make herself poorer to help him out! That meant she loved him, or at the very least felt affection for him, didn't it? André moved over to Paula, and wrapped his arm around her.

"It's very kind," he said, "but it won't be necessary. Don't worry about it."

"You're sure?"

"Absolutely sure." In truth, he wished it were only a question of money; he would have been capable of sorting it out himself. But, in fact, it wasn't money that was lacking; on the contrary, there had perhaps been too much… he repeated, tightening his embrace,

"Don't worry."

"Everyone's telling me not to worry today," said Paula, "it's very worrying."

The evening passed without trouble. In the end, they'd decided not to go out. They had a light supper and watched a film on the television, a wonderful film by François Truffaut that Paula had already seen twice, *La Femme d'à côté*. Then they went up to bed. Before they slept, they made love: not, as usual, out of obligation, and to reassure themselves that they were still a couple, but with tenderness, and a softness that reminded them of their first years together.

The next day they went back to Paris together. Paula didn't want to stay at Boyrive alone, and she'd arranged for Yvette to call if she heard anything. Arriving home, they found a bunch of flowers: an enormous bouquet of royal lilies and blue hyacinths from the renowned florist's Lachaume's, which must have cost a fortune. They had arrived the previous day and the maid had put them in a vase filled with water without taking off the cellophane. Paula read the card that accompanied the flowers: Youri, apologising for being angry on the telephone and asking if there was any news about Martine.

Sadness suddenly welled up in her.

The missing person's notice appeared in the Courrier de Seine-et-Marne the following Saturday. Paula had put in a recent photo, a portrait that she'd taken herself, and in which Martine wore her hair down to her shoulders - her face still clear and unobstructed – long, straight hair, naturally blond, very recognisable. In either case, hair down or up, she wasn't a woman who went unnoticed; if someone had seen her, they would certainly remember her. The notice was published on the last page, the most read and seen after the front page according to what she'd been told by the correspondent on the telephone. The Courrier was a morning paper, so by midday, Saturday 7th September, half of Neuville knew about the disappearance of the youngest of the Jensen sisters.

Then things got going.

The insurance agent, waiting at the Peugeot garage for his car to be brought to him, had mechanically taken one of the copies from the stack, piled next to the door. The notice jumped out at him, and he pointed it out to the garage owner who went to show it to his wife. As she knew the two sisters well, she telephoned the house in Boyrive. Since there was no response, they wondered what they could do to help. They decided to blow up the picture on the photocopier and fix it to the petrol pump, so it would be visible to all the cars that stopped by.

At the same moment, the ironmonger was in the queue at the bakers, glancing through the news items. Coming across the missing person's notice, he showed it to the baker, who, unable to leave the counter, sent her apprentice to the newsagents. The Courrier lay folded to the last page on top of the counter, feeding conversation the whole morning.

The Champion supermarket, on the road out of Neuville, had a newspaper shelf which meant that people living on the outskirts could get the news at the same time as everyone else. The hundred copies of the Courrier, which the shop received every morning, were gone within a quarter of an hour.

People flocked in from far and wide to the newsagent's in the town centre which, in no time at all, had exhausted its stock. Neuville was as animated as if it were a fair day. Those who had been able to buy a copy of the paper were stopped in the street by the less fortunate who wanted to see the photo. Groups formed on the pavement and the road – there were nearly traffic jams as a result.

Yvette was used to crowds on Saturdays, but that Saturday was like the metro at rush hour! Not knowing where to turn, she rushed to and fro in the infernal hubbub, and didn't have time to pay attention to what people were saying.

Finally, the town hall clock chimed half twelve. The waves of people subsided; in the blink of an eye the village was deserted. In Neuville, mealtimes were no laughing matter.

Paula arrived in Boyrive at the beginning of the afternoon. With all the mess she'd created, she had to be there at least, but she stayed timidly in the house. She made the most of it by catching up with the mail. Letters for her sister were piling up: invitations, bank letters, administrative reminders... for them too, it seemed as though Martine was playing dead. A postcard had arrived from Saint-Barth that Paula hoped fervently was from Martine, but it wasn't her handwriting: the card had been sent by a friend. Paula threw it into a drawer. She then examined her own mail and sorted it. Finally, she folded the newspaper that she'd bought on the way and contemplated once more the photo of her sister on the back page. She'd taken it the afternoon of the previous Christmas, on the banks of the Seine, while she'd been walking with André and Youri after the family lunch that Paula had organised for the four of them at Saint-Dominique road. It was cold, dry and sunny. After their umpteenth dispute, Martine had just gotten back together with Youri; she looked fantastic. A little tipsy after the good wine they'd drunk at lunch, they'd all taken photos of each other, alone, in pairs, three at a time, with the Tuileries gardens in the background, its trees visible from across the Seine; the kind of photos where everyone's smiling a little stupidly. They were happy, after all, and far from imagining what the photo of Martine would be used for a few months from then...

Paula took a book and went to sprawl on the sofa, next to the telephone. She hoped that in Neuville someone would remember something and that Yvette would call her.

The customers reappeared in The Old Oak at around four o'clock. They had left their copies of the Courrier at home, but didn't talk any less about the Jensen girl (some of them were already calling it 'The Jensen Affair') - it was even their principal topic of conversation.

They were all in agreement that she was something of a beauty. Moreover, both sisters were beautiful, as alike as two peas in a pod. In fact, the one in the paper, Martine, was she the elder or the younger? The younger,

Yvette told them, twenty-eight years old. They thought that twenty-eight was too young to die. She's maybe just run off with some bloke, suggested an old man. At her age, a younger man pointed out, you don't need to run off, you can go where you want. I think that she was married, said another, to a surgeon from Paris. The others told her that Martine hadn't been married for ages, that she was divorced. And you should have seen the life she led! With singers and actors, stars from the telly... you'd see them at Neuville sometimes, they'd get out from a convoy of cars, a real carnival! Once, they'd even seen Johnny Hallyday... No?! Yes. Nah, must have been his body double... He even came to the municipal rooms once, it was a right laugh. The one who was in Boyrive was the real one, he even signed a photo for my niece Paulette, she could show you. "Yes," said Yvette, "but that was before Martine's divorce, when she was still married to the surgeon." Ah, humph, said the old man.

The people of Neuville continued to arrive. Considering that it was the middle of the afternoon, there were lots of women: usually, they came for their Saturday drinks later in the day. Naturally, they knew more about the Jensen sisters than the men, especially those who were about their age and who had associated with them when they were little; some had even been invited to Boyrive for a children's tea party or a birthday party. During adolescence, they didn't see each other anymore; the Jensen girls preferred to invite their Parisian friends to Boyrive, and their friends in Neuville felt scorned. Some of them even felt resentful about it. Without admitting it, they were jealous of the two sisters for their beauty, their expensive clothes, their house, their beautiful cars, everything that they possessed. On the point of saying what they really felt, they remembered just in time that the girls had just been struck by misfortune, and they closed their mouths like carps, lips pinched against the gossip that they swallowed back.

Amongst the older women, several had known their parents, the ones who'd died in a plane accident, how awful... And to think that their father had been a banker! Well, you see, it's no use envying others when you never know what's going to happen. And now their girl... Well, what the heck was she doing there, it's not normal living like that, all alone. Supposedly doing her painting. Days and days holed up in her studio without seeing anyone... wait, she had a visitor! The thing is, she's not really the serious one, the youngest... One stated - without malice, but just to steer the younger ones – "you see what happens when you don't fit in."

They talked about the past, back as far as the grandparents, the mother's parents, the Belvoix, they were good people. When they'd bought the house in Boyrive, they'd done a lot for the community. The old man especially, he was really someone, eighteen years on the Municipal Council! A capable man... and what did those two die of?

"The question now," Yvette interrupted them, "is to find out where Martinc is at the moment. The family are going out of their minds. It's the eldest who put the notice in the paper. It's been more than two weeks with no news..."

The gossips kept quiet, nodding their heads with a saddened and doubtful air.

"Anyone here saw her at all?"

"She's someone we rarely saw, we'd notice her from time to time, that's all."

"She came two or three times to do the shopping," said a checkout assistant from the Champion, "but usually she'd have it delivered to the house."

"It'd be better to ask Manuella. She's not here?"

"Manuella's Portugese, she doesn't usually come to the café."

"I saw Martine in the market, the last Thursday in July, it was. I remember because my mother was with me, she'd come to spend three days here... the Jensen girl, she was wearing a red cap, a kind of baseball cap, it made my mother laugh."

"Well, if she still has it, it won't be hard to find her, we'll see her from a long way off!" Laughter rang out, which was just as soon interrupted, ashamed.

"Didn't she have a dog? It seems to me that there was always a dog with her."

"César," Yvette nodded, "a brown Labrador. You haven't seen it, Mauricette? No one's seen a dog walking around on its own?"

But no one had seen an errant dog.

"And there's also the car. They haven't found her car, a Peugeot 308."

"If they haven't found her dog or her car, it's because she left with them, you don't have to look any further than that."

"It's not what her sister thinks. She knows her, after all. What would you say if your sister disappeared all of a sudden without warning?"

"No chance of that. Monique would never do it. We don't do that kind of thing at ours."

"Well," said an old lady who'd been listening for a while without saying anything, "just where has this Jensen girl gone, exactly?"

At that very moment, in his office on the Balzac road, André was preparing the schedule for the cosmetics manufacturer whose business, thanks to a totally unexpected intervention – some unhoped-for support – had taken off again in Russia, and had even grown to the point where M. Rouleau had become one of his best clients. After the theft of three of their cargo loads, two VasseurTransEurope lorries, and to cap it all off the kidnapping of one of the drivers, they had really thought that the Russian market was lost to them. And then – it was just eighteen months ago – M. Rouleau had received a phone call that had sorted everything out. A telephone call sent from heaven, or at least that's what they thought at the time.

The call came from a certain Sergueï Loujkovitch, who had introduced himself as the Business Attaché of the Russian Embassy in Paris. Monsieur Loujkovitch had heard that Monsieur Rouleau was ending all exports to Russia and very respectfully asked the reason why, proposing that he make himself useful if he could. M. Rouleau, who suspected that he knew very well the reason why, since he had had to tell his clients himself why he was suspending operations, soberly replied that a number of his consignments had been hijacked. What a scandal, exclaimed M. Loujkovitch, what a shame to deny the Russian women of such excellent French products, and what an unfortunate, deplorable loss to the economy of his country! He would see what he could do.

A few days later, without announcing themselves, two distinguished men presented themselves at the factory reception. Long navy blue overcoats, dazzlingly bright white shirt collars, dark ties, with manicured nails and immaculate hands (this kind of detail wasn't lost on the trained eye of M. Rouleau). They had arrived in a black Mercedes registered to the Diplomatic Corps, which was now parked in the courtyard. Messieurs Mikhaï Loukachenko and Oleg Yakovlev presented themselves as Russian diplomats; they had been sent to him by M. Loujkovitch. Both spoke French.

The cosmetics manufacturer listened sympathetically to these men who promised to reopen the doors of their Eldorado to him – the kind of prospect that allayed his suspicions. After the usual civilities, he had taken them around the factory. The huge vats filled with scarlet paste, mixed by enormous mechanical spoons, seemed to amuse them greatly: leaning over the edge, they laughed and joked between themselves in Russian (really, there was a lot to be pleased about when you thought about the amount of dough this mixture represented once cut up into packaged sticks in pretty golden tubes). Then they came to the point: to sum up, if M. Rouleau agreed to revive his business in Russia, they proposed to have the shipments supervised by the police. Charmed, M. Rouleau took his visitors there and then to his road haulier.

The Russians had reiterated their offer in front of André. At his place, they had also shown a polite inquisitiveness; they had admired his fleet, which at the time numbered nineteen lorries in perfect condition, noting the imposing dimensions of his depot and his warehouse. Before leaving, they left a mobile number and asked that, should M. Rouleau decide to resume his deliveries to their country, to please give them a week's notice. Then they left, but not before promising to send André some clients.

As a precaution, M. Rouleau phoned the embassy and asked for M. Loujkovitch. The secretary said that he was in a meeting and would call him back: which he did, one hour later. M. Rouleau talked to him about his visitors. The other confirmed that he had sent them, but before hanging up, asked him to call on his mobile from then on, because the embassy's help was unofficial, and they didn't want this type of service to become widely known. M. Rouleau didn't think any more about it.

André wasn't naïve, he wasn't unaware of the threats that weighed on businesses like his, particularly over the course of the last decade. Road transport companies, however, were so numerous and it was such a fragmented sector that he never thought that it would happen to him, that he risked ending up one day under the thumb of the mafia. For the fifteen years that VasseurTransEurope had been going, he had never had to deal with this kind of problem. With time, he had built a reputation for integrity that was his principal asset for the big luxury brands, who made up the lion's share of his client base. In brief, until that point he had never been an outlaw.

The first moment of surprise passed, and after having talked long and hard about the proposal, André and M. Rouleau decided to go for it. After all, you can't do business without taking some risks.

André closed the Rouleau schedule book and went to move some pins on the road map fixed to his wall. He never grew tired of this mathematical game, where the loading of the cargo, the movement of the lorries, the rotation of the drivers, all had to be fine-tuned as accurately as possible - like the pieces of a three-dimensional puzzle which had to be plotted in space and time. Despite the never-ending headache of reverse logistics, so as to avoid bringing the lorries back empty, this aspect of his work had always enthralled him. And it still succeeded in making him forget his worries for a few hours.

The next day, Sunday, Yvette telephoned Paula who was still waiting in Boyrive for news. Unfortunately, despite the commotion unleashed by the publication of the missing person's notice, she didn't have anything important to tell her. No one had seen her sister, nor had anyone remarked anything out of the ordinary. People couldn't remember anything that was recent; they'd promised to think about it. Yvette hadn't counted on it. What she thought – though she kept her thoughts to herself – was that the idea that a crime could have been committed in Neuville was profoundly disturbing. There was, of course, petty crime – drunk driving, systematic burglary of isolated houses, destruction of ATM's, seizure of small drug stocks - without adding kidnapping, rape, assassination, or all three at once into the mix, the idea of which terrified the community and the surrounding hamlets. They wouldn't find out anything because no one wanted to know. And if something bad had happened to the Jensen girl, it would be better for everyone if it had happened elsewhere, far from Neuville and its inhabitants.

CHAPTER 4.

Gaston Colin woke up at five in the morning and switched off the buzzer on his alarm clock - set to go off at half five – so as not to wake his wife, who was still sleeping. It was Sunday; she was allowed to rest a little. He got up and looked out of the window: it was still dark, of course, but dry and the forecast was sunny.

Showering rapidly, he slipped on the clothes that he'd laid out the previous evening and went down to the kitchen. He'd just lit the gas under the cafetière when he heard the footsteps of his son on the stairs. He had also woken before his alarm; hunting was a passion he shared with his father, and he didn't want to be late. The door opened.

"Morning, Dad."

"Morning, son. Coffee's brewing."

Gaston put the loaf of bread, the cheese and the sausage on the table while François laid out the bowls and the cutlery. Father and son got on well together. François Colin was thirty-five years old, single, and had never moved out of his parents' house - unlike his younger brother who ran a garage in Melun, and his sister who had married a man working for 'Electricité de France' and lived in Nemours. In any case, the Gaston's farm couldn't have supported everyone. It was the last farm in Vaucerf, a hamlet in Neuville, like Boyrive, but situated on the opposite side. A small farm of eighty hectares – corn, oats, and oilseed rape – next to nothing compared with the immense undertakings in neighbouring Beauce; it sufficed, just about, for three people.

François turned down the gas under the cafetière, which had started to whistle.

"You want milk?" he asked, pouring some coffee for his father.

"I'd prefer a drop of something stronger," said Gaston, "it's not going to get warm for a while."

François brought over the plum brandy and sat opposite him.

"We'll have to sort out the sandwiches."

"Mother prepared them last night, they're in the pantry. We'll take them when we go."

They swallowed their breakfast in silence, already savouring the pleasure of the morning that lay ahead of them. For more than twenty years, they'd been hunting together; the first time François had been fourteen, and he mused that - apart from a holiday in Germany during his youth - he'd never missed a single season. The weather looked promising. The guns had been properly greased, the cartridges were ready, patiently filled by Gaston who had his own recipe and liked to make them himself. In the courtyard, the dogs - who had been watching the preparations for two days now - pulled on their leashes, barking enough to wake the whole district. François went out to feed them.

It was the opening of the hunting season, which this year had been fixed for the fifteenth of September.

As always, the Colins set out on foot: they didn't mind the two mile hike; on the contrary, it limbered up their legs and they would arrive in the forest of Boisregard at sunrise. The dogs, ecstatic, had at first danced at their feet, jumping and yapping around them, but they quickly adjusted their rhythm to the regular pace of their masters - except for a few instances when they became impatient and set off running ahead, turning their heads back towards them, inviting them to hurry too. They were two Brittany spaniels, two beautiful white males with red spots, athletic and playful – a father and son, as well. "This way," said Gaston, "we hunt as a family!" The dogs responded to the names of Bandit and Boy. François had mated Bandit with a beautiful spaniel bitch, in exchange for which her mistress had let them choose a pup from the litter: a good breed.

Day was breaking when they reached Boisregard. François glanced around the meadow that bordered the forest on the right. They couldn't see any preparations being made.

"Didn't Monsieur Thibaut invite anyone for the opening day of the season?"

"No," said Gaston, "he's on holiday. So I've been told."

Mr Thibaut, a businessman from Paris who owned a country house in Vaucerf, had rented six hectares of hunting ground from the owner in the region. On days when Mr Thibaut hunted, the Colins, walking by in the small hours, could see the game wardens preparing the ground and putting up the look-outs. The businessman and his guests, however, never came before nine o'clock. When walking back about midday, their satchels full, the Colins would see them - these Parisian hunters - lined up on the edge of the meadow, two steps from their station wagons and their 4x4's. Crouched behind their low straw hide-outs, all they had to do was wait for the rabbits, tracked down and flushed out of the forest by the beaters, panic-stricken creatures rushing out only to get killed in a hail of gunfire. But, even like this, (and the countryside folk couldn't help but laugh about it), they still couldn't hit them! They had to ask for help from the game wardens! Which is just about acceptable when it's a wild rabbit... but then you had to see the pheasants! Pheasants raised in captivity, imported from Central Europe or God-knows-where, released into the forest a week before, and who approached the cars calmly believing that they were going to be fed. You'd never seen friendlier game! "They might as well go shooting at the fair," Gaston considered, "it would cost them less." But father and son contented themselves with joking to each other, since Mr Thibaut wasn't a bad bloke, and invited them along sometimes to add to the spoils of the hunt. And at his house, they did excellent blow-out feasts! Not to mention the people you met there, Gaston once even talked to a Minister.

It was well known that the Colins were the best shots in the country; the two of them had once managed to shoot a dozen creatures in one morning... to think what they could bring back in one season! They kept the best for the farm, with which Madame Colin made stews and pâtés, and sold the rest to Yvette and to the Hôtel de la Poste.

Since the land to the right of the road was private hunting ground, the Colins turned to the left and entered the communal forest. They were welcomed by the beating of crows' wings: the crows, having spotted their guns, flew off shrieking to warn their fellow creatures. They pushed deeper into the woods, avoiding crackling the leaves too much under their feet, smelling the scents of the earth and the moss that the dampness of the dawn had rendered more pungent. Each time they hunted, especially the first day of the season, father and son were gripped by the same emotion, which they shared without knowing how to explain it. It was a solid bond between them - the love of the hunt, yes, but more than that – an understanding of the countryside, a profound affinity with nature. Their dogs ran ahead, sniffing, retracing their steps, sifting through the bushes, two peerless scruffs, without equal in their ability to flush game out of their hiding places and into the sights of their masters. And crack! Once seen, the animal had no chance, a Colin rarely missed his target. Bandit and Boy, tough and hardy beasts, were also excellent fetchers, adept at finding a bird that had fallen far away. As Gaston's father (who was also a reputed hunter) always used to say, a good dog is worth as much as a good gun.

Despite everything, the first part of the morning was mediocre. By ten o'clock, they'd only caught a wild rabbit, killed by François. They'd seen a wild boar pass a hundred meters away, which was probably what was chasing the game off. Tired, they sat on a trunk to have something to eat while their dogs lay at their feet, ready to catch any scraps of meat that Madame Colin had prepared, since they'd also spent a lot of energy and had to regain their strength.

"What did Mother make us?" said Gaston, opening his satchel (he called his wife 'Mother' as if, throughout the years, she'd become mother to both of them), "ham and goats' cheese... and as for the wine, she's measured it a little short, there's only just enough for a small glass each!"

"That's enough for the morning, Dad, you don't wanna overdo it... Did you see the wild boar earlier, he must have weighed at least two hundred kilos."

"A pig like that, I'd rather see him from far-off than close-up!"

"He frightened off the rabbits, we'd do better going elsewhere," suggested François. He bit into his sandwich, scrutinising the countryside around them.

"Mother asked us to bring back mushrooms if we see any," said Gaston.

"Don't call her 'Mother' all the time, you know she doesn't like it."

"Sylviane. Some boletus mushrooms, she'd like that."

"It hasn't rained enough yet, and it's not a boletus area here, I've never seen any... Sylviane, that means 'she of the forest,' did you know that? I read it in the Almanac."

"Well, it suits her then, doesn't it?!" said Gaston. "How about we go and have a look near the Drift? There's a lot of game over there."

François thought it was a great idea.

"There's no lack of clearings that way, we might see a hare."

"And we'll look for mushrooms for Moth... for your Mother at the same time."

Their sandwiches finished, and being men who respected the forest, they folded their greasy papers in a plastic bag which they put back in their satchels, and began walking again. The dogs went back to work with enthusiasm, running, scratching and sniffing the undergrowth; they walked like that for a over half a mile. Suddenly, fifty meters ahead, Bandit and Boy came to a stand-still. François first believed that they'd seen a rabbit, but instead of going to flush it out, they ran back at full tilt to their masters, barking and whimpering. Gripped by a sense of grim foreboding, Gaston and his son stood still. At that moment, the dogs, still barking and jumping around them, ran ahead a few meters, then came back to nip at their trouser legs, bringing them to see the discovery. The Colins decided to follow them.

Approaching the place where the dogs, who had gone ahead, had stopped again, they were hit by the nauseating odour of rotting flesh. Handkerchiefs to their noses, they moved forward another few steps: half-covered by the bushes, but close to the path, as if someone had dragged it to the thicket without bothering to cover it up, was a body, partially eaten by forest animals, ripped open, the bowels teeming with insects, which must have been there for days... a large dog, from what they could see, a brown Labrador. At least, what remained of it.

The hunt stopped there. Looking at the poor beast, Gaston remembered having heard his wife discussing something with the neighbours a few days ago: a girl, they were talking about a girl, from Neuville, who'd disappeared. That afternoon, he'd been working in the corn with François and couldn't waste any time: he had to take the corn-picker back two days later, as he shared it with another farmer. He'd only breezed into the house to get a tool that he needed, and hadn't paid much attention to the women's chatter. But now, the bits and pieces that he'd been able to pick up from their conversation came back to him.

On the path home, he talked briefly about it with his son, who hadn't known anything about it and didn't understand why his father had interrupted their hunt.

"The dog could've been attacked by a wild boar."

"Maybe, but what the hell was he doing there on his own?"

"A stray dog..."

"We'll see." Gaston thought about it, "It's still a coincidence," he said, "that girl... and now this dog. It's not often that you find dead dogs in that area, especially a pedigree. Maybe it was her dog, we'll see. I'd like to talk to the gendarmes about it."

Seeing them come into the kitchen, Madame Colin was startled.

"Already?" She caught sight of the flat satchels that they threw on the table, and took out the rabbit from one of them, "is that all?" She felt its weight with an expert hand, holding it by the ears, "it's not even two kilos," and added "you've come back too early, lunch isn't ready yet." Then she noticed that they weren't taking off their coats.

"We're off again," said Gaston, "I have to talk to the gendarmes. We found something."

"What then?"

"Weren't you talking the other day about a missing girl, a girl from around here?"

His wife paled and dropped onto a chair.

"You found the Jensen girl?"

"No," said François, "we just found a dog."

"A dog, well, she had one from what I heard. But I couldn't tell you what breed."

"We found a Labrador," said Gaston, "and it wasn't fresh. Well, let's go, I'm taking your car, we'll just pop there and back."

As it was a Sunday, the gendarmerie was closed. The service number was tacked to the door. François came back to the car and took out his mobile.

"You think it's the right time to call him? He must be about to eat."

"It doesn't matter," said Gaston, "call him, he'll be here in five minutes."

"For a dog," said François, "you, once you've got something in your head…"

Brigadier Boivin joined them, buttoning up his jacket. Gaston explained the affair to him and he also made the connection with the disappearance in Boyrive.

Unfortunately, the Brigadier Chief wasn't there; he was on leave for two days and had gone with his family to visit his in-laws. He wouldn't be there until the next morning. The Brigadier reflected: right then, it was just a dog, and it was lunchtime - Sunday lunch - his wife and his children were waiting for him to join them at the table. He advised his visitors to go and have lunch, and to meet up that afternoon.

At three o'clock, Brigadier Boivin arrived at the Colin farm, accompanied by Brigadier Perrault. Gaston and François got into the gendarmes' car and guided them to the communal forest path they'd taken that morning, in the direction of the wood around the Drift. As it was suitable to drive, the brigadiers carried on, stopping, on Colin's indication, at the beginning of the narrow track where the dog's corpse lay a hundred meters further on. They left the car and walked the rest on foot.

Once there, their handkerchief against their mouths, they lent over the dog.

"Ugh…"

"Well?" said Gaston, as if proud of his find.

"It's a Labrador?" said Boivin, "You're sure?"

"Yes, yes, it's a Labrador."

François, realising that the brigadiers were taking his father seriously, confirmed, "A brown Labrador, and a good size."

"From what the Brigadier Chief said, it's that kind of breed that she had, the missing girl?" Boivin asked his colleague.

"Yep, that's what he said."

They'd stepped back a few paces to get away from the stench, and gazed at the corpse skeptically.

"What do we do?" said Boivin.

"We'll have to take it," said Perrault after a moment's reflection, "we can't leave it here. The annoying thing is that it's Sunday, we're not going to see anyone about it today. Anyway, go get the bag that's in the car," he said, "and bring a rope. We'll use it to mark the boundary just in case there are tracks to pick up." He looked at the leaves and the broken branches strewn over the ground. "Of course, given the length of time, there's no certainty we'll find anything."

"You can see the trail where he was dragged," François intervened, "the grass is flattened there, see, on the right. If he'd been hurt, there'll be blood somewhere."

Brigadier Boivin was already running up the path.

"Don't forget the camera," Perrault called out to him.

While waiting, the three men examined the clearing, hoping to find a button, a piece of fabric caught on a branch, a cigarette butt, incriminating evidence of any kind, but without success. The brushwood had swallowed its secrets.

Boivin was back, they took photos and all there was left to do was to place the lifeless animal into the bag. Hesitating, the brigadiers considered the rotting carcass with repugnance, not knowing which end to pick it up.

"I could help," suggested François.

"No, no! Above all, don't touch anything."

One unfolded the bag and held it open, while the other, lifting the animal by two of its paws, roughly threw it into the opening. Then, with the help of pegs improvised from bits of wood, they stretched the rope out to form quite a large perimeter around the area where the animal was found.

"Did the dog have a collar?" Gaston asked.

"They must have taken it off," said Perrault, "and gotten rid of it elsewhere."

"This whole thing is worrying," said François, suddenly remembering the young missing woman.

The gendarmes fell silent, wiping their hands with their handkerchiefs.

"That's not all," said Gaston, "now we have to look for the girl."

Suddenly, gunfire started to ring out in bursts on all sides.

"Shit, the hunters!" Boivin cried out, "We don't want to stay here."

The gendarmes quickly gathered up the bag and everyone ran to the car.

Driving back to Neuville after dropping the Colins at their farm, they asked each other what they should do with the carcass. The authorised veterinary police services were in Melun, which was a sixty mile drive there and back. Perrault had invited some friends over for a drink that evening, and it was nearly the end of the afternoon. On the other hand, it was a delicate situation: the dog's corpse was incriminating evidence and they didn't want to dispose of it without the approval of their supervisor. They ended up telling themselves that it would have been better to leave it where it was and not to have touched it.

"We could maybe call the Chief," suggested Boivin.

'Yeah, so he thinks I'm an idiot,' thought Perrault, and said "There's the funeral home, we can get the keys from the Town Hall."

"But it's closed on a Sunday, the Town Hall... and a dog in a funeral home!"

There was one other possibility. The gendarmes who made up the unit in Neuville lived with their families in the barracks, and, while waiting for the Brigadier Chief to come back, evidently the simplest thing would be to keep the bag with them. But neither of them could see themselves asking their wives to empty the fridge to allow a lifeless dog to spend the night in it.

"What if we called the vet?" said Boivin, "he must have a cool room, a kind of funeral home for animals."

"Good idea," said Perrault, "and tomorrow the whole godforsaken village will know about it." He suddenly looked pensive, "There's the butcher, he has a refrigerated room, we can put it there with the slices of meat."

"Eh!"

"Oh come on, I'm joking."

"In the end," Boivin declared, "we would have been better off leaving it where it was."

"We could take it back, if you want. But you'll keep guard over it all night."

"If it was winter," Boivin hastened to add, "we could have put it in the courtyard."

"Yep, but it's September, and it's still warm even now," said Perrault.

In any case, remembering that the nights were cool, that was the option they decided to take: they covered the bag with a tarpaulin sheet, and left it in the back courtyard of the barracks, as far as possible from the apartment windows.

Monday morning, Brigadier Chief Gallard, having yelled heartily at them, sent his men to take the thing double-quick to the veterinary services of the police in Melun. Then he called Paula Jensen in Paris to ask her to come and identify the carcass.

Two and a half hours later, Paula arrived at the address provided. Out of consideration for the family, and very conscious of the worrying significance of the macabre discovery, the Brigadier Chief had gone over in person.

"It's César," she said, when they showed her the animal, "he had that mark on his front paw." She teetered, but refused the chair he offered her.

"You're certain?"

"Absolutely. I would have recognised him anywhere – just by his head."

"The veterinary surgeon has concluded," said one of the policemen present, "that the dog was strangled."

Brigadier Chief Gallard accompanied Paula, supporting her until she reached the car: her legs could literally hold her no more.

"We're going to help you," he said, realising that she was thinking about what might have happened to her sister. "I will meet you shortly in my office, from two o'clock. We'll record your statement, and we'll open a preliminary enquiry. Rest assured that we will do everything in our power," he concluded, gently closing the door to the 508.

A search was organised for the next day. They began at dawn, around the area where they'd found the dog. From the outskirts of the communal forest to the edges of the woods around the Drift, there were about nine hundred hectares to rake over. That first day, ten of them took part: the gendarmes Perrault and Boivin, three firemen, a dog-handler with his German Shepherd, lent by the police in Melun, two volunteer game wardens, and of course, the Colins, who had discovered the animal and knew the forest like the back of their hands. Nine hundred hectares of dense undergrowth and thicket to explore: in other words, the first search boiled down to doing some reconnaissance.

But for all that, they really drove out some game! Walking forward in a line, ten meters apart from one another, they flushed out dozens of rabbits and pheasants that proceeded to run like mad in all directions. Those of the participants who had taken a gun clasped the gun-butts - how frustrating, they wouldn't have minded shooting one or two, but, oh well, they weren't there to have fun. At the end of the morning, exhausted, having agreed to meet there again at two o'clock, they went back to their cars and returned home.

With the permission of the owner - the farmer who was letting his hunting ground to Mr Thibaut - the afternoon was dedicated to searching the ground situated to the right-hand side of the road. There were bushy groves, yes, but also harvested fields, great uncovered stretches that you could take in at a glance. The police dog, who they'd got to smell one of Martine Jensen's pullovers, worked hard. He flew through the fields, sniffing, scratching, going into the woods to rummage through the bushes. At times he came back to his handler - tired and ashamed at coming back empty-handed - who got him to smell the jumper once more, and lavished lots of encouragement on him. The men didn't skimp in their efforts either, but still it was in vain. By mid-afternoon, worn out and discouraged, they took a break.

"Perhaps there's no need to look over there," said one of the game wardens.

"That's right," said the other, "and it's not because the dog was found there. Whoever did that wanted to separate the dog from the girl. The body of the girl on one side, the corpse of the dog on the other. To blur the trail, delay the search."

"Hang on," said Brigadier Perrault, "we don't know yet that she's been killed."

"That's true," remarked a fireman, "it's a good thing that we can't find her."

"And then there's the car," said François, "her car hasn't been found either. And it can't have vanished into thin air."

"The murderer could have rolled it into a pond," suggested the second game warden, "it's marshy enough in this area."

"Especially since it's not a big car, a Peugeot 308."

"And the Essonne... maybe he tossed it into the Essonne."

"It's very deep around here."

"Or maybe just the girl... maybe she was drowned."

"Or maybe the car is in the river with the girl inside it," Gaston summed up.

"We can guess at anything," Perrault cut in, "the thing is that we don't have a lead."

Even so, he sent the dog-handler and the dog to finish the day off on the banks of the Essonne and promised himself he'd secure the services of Melun's police to explore the river with a diver, at least up to the lock thirty kilometres further down. Then they resumed the search, which lasted until nightfall.

The next morning everyone met at the house in Boyrive. They had decided to continue their search on the outskirts of the property. They were a few more people than the previous day; three more volunteers had signed up for the search. As the gendarmes Perrault and Boivin were on duty elsewhere, Brigadier Chief Gallard replaced them, accompanied by a young gendarme who completed the brigade. Paula was present at the meeting place. Even though he had already spoken to her on the telephone the previous evening, the Brigadier explained again where they were.

"You see," he concluded, "we're putting our resources into it."

Paula was sceptical.

"And what about a helicopter?" she said.

Gallard knew that no-one was going to provide him with a helicopter. It wasn't a missing child. And for the moment, they hadn't found any hard evidence – an item of clothing, for example, a scrap of material, a drop of human blood – to make them think that the woman had been murdered.

"Above the woods, a helicopter wouldn't be of much use," he responded.

Paula asked to help with the search, and they tried to dissuade her. She insisted. She thought that if her sister were close to the house, she would feel it, that a kind of energy linked them and would lead her to Martine. Completely irrational. But, after their departure, and even before they'd reached the edge of the Boyrive wood, something unexpected happened. Sometimes members of the same family, especially brothers or sisters, have the same bodily smell. The police dog, who had been given Martine's jumper to smell, went straight over to Paula and stopped in front of her, barking and preventing her from moving forward.

Paula realised that she would hold up the search, and resigned herself to going back to the house, torn by opposing sentiments. On the one hand, she believed that they weren't doing everything they could to find her sister, and on the other hand, after the terror that she'd felt seeing César, disembowelled, the fact that they hadn't found Martine until now reassured her a little. It allowed her some hope.

The others had recommenced the search, they were more numerous now, but lacked conviction. The fact that there was no hard evidence to serve as a guide meant that there was no special reason to examine one particular place or another. At this rate, they might as well have divided up the whole of France. The police dog hadn't found anything on the banks of the Essonne. A driver had been arranged for the next day, but it had been nearly a month since the girl had vanished, and motivation was crumbling. Those who'd been looking since the previous day showed signs of weariness, the eldest were puffing hard, and they were forced to take breaks more and more frequently. Won over by the discouraging mood, the new participants also dragged their heels. They kept at it until midday and then ended the search.

For the gendarmes, the difficult part was to come. They would have to go door-to-door through Neuville and the surrounding areas to try and gather information. The local residents, of course, wouldn't slam the door in their faces - as they probably would if it were, for instance, a door-to-door salesman - but they didn't like seeing the gendarmes come to nose about their homes. The gendarmes knew why: the inhabitants of Neuville, whilst honest citizens, were experts in getting things for free. Some of them poached, which ranged from simply putting down snares or lines - child's play really - to hunting game at night, which was strictly forbidden. If they hadn't already sold them to the butchers to make pâté, you could easily find large cuts of venison stowed in their freezers, as though they were stocking up for winter. Others, those who weren't hunters, did up their houses: they installed extra bathrooms, changed their attics into spare rooms or games rooms, all the while forgetting to inform the property tax service of these improvements. The more enterprising even went as far as building workshops, modestly called 'garden sheds', or even the 'second garage', soon topped with a second floor, without planning permission. Consequently, there had arisen a black market for the exchange of services, each providing something according to his talents. But where the inhabitants of Neuville demonstrated a remarkable ingenuity, was in the connection and diversion of water mains (before they arrived at the meter), a real headache for the distribution company which recorded huge disparities between the volume of water taken from the wells and what was billed to consumers, without ever being able to find the guilty parties.

The gendarmes were perfectly well aware of these violations (and often were tipped off by the inhabitants themselves). But, in addition to numbering among those things that didn't directly concern them, it wasn't what was keeping them busy for the moment. Brigadiers Perrault and Boivin, who had been charged with leading the search, undertook their door-to-door visits with tact, keeping themselves to the threshold of the door as much as possible, or even the garden gate, and facing away from the house so as to put their interlocutors at ease.

Despite this precaution, they still drew a blank. Instead of gathering information, they were almost scolded; after all, they were responsible for maintaining law and order, they were paid to do so. The fear that had pervaded the village made its inhabitants aggressive. As soon as the gendarmes moved off, mothers - who had never before had the opportunity to speak publicly - seized the opportunity to make their voices heard: "It's shameful," they shouted in the middle of the street, pulling their children closely to them, "you have to ask why such horrors are allowed to happen! Do your jobs! Arrest the murderer!" Spitefully inflaming the situation, they rounded up their neighbours - it was nearly touch and go whether the women would band together and chase after them... as if, instead of a dog, it had been the corpse of the Jensen girl that they had discovered, when they didn't even know if she had been killed! It must be noted that the measures taken (with the approbation of the Mayor, in memory of the grandfather who had done so much for the community) - the search, the diver (who hadn't found anything either), the quest for information undertaken door-to-door, certainly gave the impression that Martine had been murdered. The two gendarmes followed orders but, in their heart of hearts, judged the reaction out of proportion.

The last day, weary, they pushed open the door of The Old Oak. At least here, the owner of the establishment was a reasonable person with whom you could have a sensible conversation. It was the middle of the afternoon and the café was calm. Seeing them, Yvette came out of the kitchen, guessing what had brought them. They greeted her politely. They wanted to know, above anything – like everyone who passed by – if she had heard anything about the affair, or noticed any odd behaviour from any of her customers. In fact, Yvette found that people were starting to look askance at one another. There was a lot of bad-mouthing: old grievances were starting to resurface. She had even surprised herself by wondering about a vagrant, an agricultural worker who was passing through, or even about a respectable member of the community, a family man that no-one would have dreamed of suspecting...

"Can I offer you anything, officers? A glass of white?" (As they were working, they only accepted a small coffee). "No," she replied in answer to their question, "I haven't seen anything out of the ordinary. People talk about it, of course, but it's nothing but a load of blah-blah, gossiping about the family. If you ask my opinion, at least about those going through the café, I'd say they don't know anything at all." She added, "But it's starting to turn sour, this whole thing, it's poisoning the atmosphere. It's about time it was all finished with."

In her own way, she was also putting them under pressure.

Once the gendarmes had gone, Yvette picked up the cups and wiped the counter. She thought about the rabbits that she'd bought off some hunters that very morning and which were gently simmering in a large stew-pot. She was preparing a "gibelotte," a wine fricassee; it wasn't complicated and was always a hit: garlic, dry white wine, with a large pinch of thyme sprinkled over the top. The smell was filling the kitchen already. With her gibelotte, she would serve a frying pan full of mushrooms. For the moment, there was only one client in the café, sat at a table in the middle of the room, an old retired labourer who usually spent his afternoons at The Old Oak, and was already on his third Ricard.

"I saw it, I did!" he suddenly called out, as Yvette was walking back to the stove.

"You saw what?"

"The Jensen girl's car. I know it, it's a black car."

"It's navy blue, Martine Jensen's car is," said Yvette.

"Eh? Well what did I say it was? That was it, a dark car."

"And just when did you see it?"

"Well I wouldn't know exactly. Maybe three or four weeks ago. I was in Boyrive visiting Nicholas, who had his sciatica."

"You don't remember what day?"

"The day? Nah," then he reflected, "it was about seven-thirty, eight, and I'd hung around to keep him company. Then I was going home for dinner."

"Maybe it wasn't hers, that car. There's enough 308's around."

"Not many cars like that over there, though. I saw it, I tell you! It was coming out of the lane that leads to the house. It was a Peugeot, a small one."

"Are you sure, Bébert?"

"I know a Peugeot when I see one!" He paused for a moment, saving the best until last, "And whadda you know, it wasn't her driving."

Yvette froze.

"Who was it then?"

"A man… well-to-do, 'e was… not someone from 'round here. I got a good look at him, I was on my bike."

"And Martine Jensen, was she with him in the car?"

"No, he was all alone."

"You're sure?"

"I'm not blind, I've still got eyes in me head!"

"If you saw something, Bébert, you must tell the gendarmes."

"What for! So they can give me hassle?"

Yvette didn't press the matter. These old country folk were more stubborn than their mules. She went back into the kitchen, promising herself to try again when he was sober.

The next day, bringing him his first Ricard, all smiles, she sat opposite him, on the pretext that she was taking a break.

"How're you, Bébert?"

"I'm well."

"Me, I'd like to go on holiday. I'm starting to feel exhausted."

"What's stopping you then? Do it."

"With the café, it's not easy. While we're on it, I've been thinking about what you told me yesterday..."

"I didn't say anything, I didn't," Bébert replied.

"You know very well what you said, about the car that you saw..."

"Ah, no, I didn't see anything."

"Hang on a second, you remember what you told me -"

"I don't remember a thing."

" - that you'd seen someone in the 308."

Bébert felt scared; just then he regretted having a big mouth and worried that Yvette might tell the gendarmes what he'd said. So he suddenly got his memory back.

"Ah, but it was just talk," he said, "to show off. A load of rubbish, y'know, for a laugh."

"Well, you had me for a while, you," said Yvette.

And she couldn't get anything more out of him.

The inhabitants of Neuville then waited for the gendarmes to act. The day after their visit to The Old Oak, they got down to questioning potential witnesses. Madame Perreira, being an employee of the Jensens, was called in first. She arrived, trembling, at the gendarmerie. Brigadier Perrault explained that she was one of the last people to see Martine Jensen, and asked her to relate, in as much detail as possible, where she was and what she'd done during the week of her disappearance. Manuella did so with bad grace, during which the young gendarme from the brigade, sat in front of his antiquated Merovingian typewriter, typed out her statement. As for the house in Boyrive, she had worked as usual on the Tuesday morning in the main building, and in the afternoon in the wing of the house where she had cleaned Madame Martine's bathroom and bedroom. She had come back on Thursday to prepare her employers' rooms, as they were due to come that weekend (although in the end, Madame Paula came alone), and she came back on Saturday morning to cook the meals.

"When you were in the wing, did you speak to Martine Jensen?"

"Yes, I spoke to her. I already told you that when you came to my house the other day. She was in the middle of painting downstairs. She didn't want me to come and clean the studio because it would disturb her work."

"She wasn't alone?"

"I don't know! I didn't go into the studio. I'd gone into the wing through the main house, by the corridor on

112

the first floor. It's Madame Martine who came upstairs to talk to me in the bedroom."

"And you didn't hear anything?"

"I've already told you, no!" She started to get angry, impressed by the metallic striking of the old Remington that the gendarme operated with two fingers. She could already see herself in front of a tribunal, like on television. "I don't even know why you've made me come! I already told you everything the other day!"

"Calm down, Madame," said Perrault, "you're here to testify as a witness"

"I can't be a witness, since I'm telling you that I didn't see anything!"

She burst into tears. Having arrived in France thirty years earlier, Manuella still hadn't quite understood that, since then, she'd become a European citizen. Her intention was to stay another seven years in the country before quietly spending her retirement in Porto, near to her son who owned the restaurant. She was afraid that, if she were mixed up in this whole awful affair, it would prevent her from finishing up her career in France, and that she would be sent back to her country prematurely.

"And the Thursday, when you came back, you didn't see anything?"

"Nothing at all! I've got enough to do without worrying about other people!"

At that moment, she remembered that in Neuville she'd heard people talking about a car, a kind of racing car that was seen by Morel the plumber in the courtyard at Boyrive. She took out her handkerchief, noisily blew her nose, and added,

"On the Wednesday, the plumber came to repair Madame Paula's bathroom. Maybe he saw something..."

Perrault continued with the interview for a further few minutes, and then put an end to her ordeal. After her statement was read aloud to her, she was made to sign it.

Manuella left the gendarmerie sniffing and dabbing at her eyes.

"And once more, they're all going to think I'm an ogre," the Brigadier said to himself.

Soon after, the gendarmes called Pierre Morel, the plumber. It was the first time they'd seen him: when they'd presented themselves at his gate during their door-to-door investigations, he wasn't there as he was working on a building site. As Paula Jensen had talked about him to the Brigadier Chief, they already knew that he'd seen a car that didn't belong to the family - a Ferrari the day he'd worked in Boyrive. They asked him for a detailed account: what time did he arrive, what time did he leave, was the Ferrari still there when he left, did he see the owner, etc. Morel repeated what he'd told Paula Jensen, adding the required information: he had arrived at two-thirty in the afternoon, after getting the house keys from Nicholas, and he had left at four: the Ferrari was still there. He had brought back the keys and went straight to the school to service the plumbing before the term started. He had worked at the school from four twenty to six o'clock - the caretaker had helped him and could verify his story. His work done for the day, he had headed home; at six-twenty, he'd arrived. It was all easy to check on, and in any case, the gendarmes didn't have any suspicions about Morel - if indeed, they had any suspicions about anyone - he was a well-regarded craftsman, not a drinker, and a father of four.

Strictly speaking, after him they should have spoken to Sammy Moore, the owner of the famous car, but they didn't want to disturb someone so well-known without a valid reason - since they still had no hard evidence concerning the missing woman - as it risked backfiring on them.

Instead, they called in Nicholas, the gardener, whom they'd already seen and who once again told them his sciatica story. The week in question, he was practically immobilised during the day, and slept under the influence of sleeping pills at night. Several people had visited him. His son had come on the Sunday and had come twice during the week to get his prescription and bring him some food. He'd also seen the plumber, who had borrowed and brought back the keys to Boyrive. Madame Paula breezed by on the Saturday. And Bébert had also visited, he didn't know which day, but he remembered that the doctor came the same morning, they only had to ask him. Bébert stayed until quarter-to-eight...

Bébert! Bébert the alcoholic! Finally, something new, the gendarmes told themselves. They cut the gardener's statement short and, once he'd left, started by telephoning the doctor's practice to get a precise idea of the day of his visit to Nicholas. Having consulted his diary, the secretary gave them the hoped-for response: the doctor had gone to see the gardener for a consultation on Wednesday 21st August at nine o'clock. The logical deduction was that Bébert was in the forest the night of Martine Jensen's disappearance. Already congratulating themselves on their intuition, the gendarmes were exultant. They only had to call in Albert Noirot - otherwise known as Bébert. With him, the only problem was when. In the afternoon, he'd already be drunk and would talk nonsense. Early in the morning, he might be out of sorts. From ten o'clock, half-ten, when he'd already drunk just two or three glasses but no more, and just before he sat down for a bite to eat, there was a narrow window where you could find him at his best. The gendarmes decided on eleven o'clock.

The next day, Bébert arrived, showered, with his hair slicked back and wearing a clean shirt - it was Thursday, but he'd dressed up as best he could as though it were Sunday. He seemed in a good mood.

"Good morning Bébert," said Perrault, holding out his hand.

"Good morning, Brigadier," he sat down without being asked and looked at the two gendarmes through cunning eyes. Boivin had replaced the youngest gendarme at the typewriter.

"Do you know why we've asked you to come?"

"Would it, by any chance, be about the Jensen girl? It's all they're talking about round here."

"Yes, it's about her," said Perrault.

"Okay then, have you found her?" asked Bébert, as though mocking them.

Vexed, Perrault changed his tone.

"We know you were at Nicholas' house on the afternoon of the 21st August," he replied sharply, "what did you do when leaving his place?"

"Well, I went to eat."

"You didn't go and have a drink at The Old Oak first?"

"I don't remember," said Bébert. "No, I came back to eat. It was already late."

"What time was it?"

"Around eight o'clock."

"You'd had a few with Nicholas?"

"Nicholas had taken his medicine. He couldn't drink."

"He offered you a glass, even so?"

"I don't remember. Maybe."

"How did you get back?"

"I had my bike with me."

"Which way did you go?"

"Took the shortcut, of course."

"You mean through the woods?"

"The path through the woods, yes."

"Did you by any chance encounter Martine Jensen?"

Bébert, who had first of all believed that Yvette had gone and told the gendarmes what he'd told her - that the evening in question he'd seen the missing girl's 308 and that it wasn't her driving it - and had come intending to waylay them and amuse himself a little before telling them what he'd seen, suddenly had the impression that they suspected him. That wiped the smile off his face.

"If I had seen her I would have said, since everyone is looking for her."

"You would have said, you would have said... that depends."

"Uh, that depends on what?"

"She's something of a beauty, that could have given you ideas. In the heat of the moment, you can do things that you later regret."

"You're crazy!" cried out Bébert, who was starting to get angry.

"Be careful," said Boivin, "before you insult a police officer."

" - but at my age? What are you thinking of!"

"When you've drunk too much, you don't really know what you're doing anymore," said Perrault.

"And what would I do with a great big gal like her? She's a head taller than me!"

"So you saw her close up?"

"So what, they're well known, both the sisters... They're like these girls nowadays that you'd think were basketball players, they can't even get through doors!"

"But if you have a gun..."

Bébert pulled himself together. He had fought in the war: not even fifteen, he had been in the Resistance. A gendarme, practically a child who was forty years his junior, was not going to scare him.

"I have no gun," he said, "I'm not a huntsman. And as for the Jensen girl, I didn't see her. There, we're talking about nothing."

"Don't you mind about that, that's for us to decide," said Perrault.

"Have to find her before you can go 'round accusing everybody," said Bébert.

Perrault thumped the desk with his fist.

"It's exactly in order to find her that we're questioning people!"

And he started up with his questions again, the same old tune, repeating himself. Since they didn't mention the 308, Bébert concluded that Yvette hadn't told them anything yet. Ah well, since they were annoying him, he wouldn't tell them anything! He declared to Perrault that he had told them everything he knew - and stopped answering. From that moment, it was impossible to get anything further out of him. He stared at a point on the floor, stubborn as an old countryman can be: it was about as much use as talking to a wall. Weary, the gendarmes sent him home.

The following morning, picking up a homeless man on the banks of the Essonne, the gendarmes forcibly escorted him to the gendarmerie. The man was already drunk. They offered him a sandwich and made him drink two cups of coffee to sober him up. Jovial at first, and then becoming more and more worried as his drunkenness wore off, the man gave his name, nationality and date of birth. He told them that he had just arrived from Normandy where he was on holiday...

"You were on holiday?" Boivin was surprised.

"In Mont Saint-Michel - there's lots of tourists there."

"So, mooching in La Manche?" said Perrault, who had mastered the names of the French districts.

"Ha, that's good one!" exclaimed Boivin.

- He was passing through Neuville for the first time, he'd never stolen anything from anyone, his record was clean, and he had stopped being interested in women ever since his todger had stopped working.

"Well that doesn't prove anything," remarked Boivin, perceptively, "sometimes it creates the exact opposite effect, and makes a man violent."

Fortunately for him, the poor man had a solid alibi: from the 18th to the 27th August, he was at the Central University Hospital in Caen, where they'd operated on his stomach. He rummaged in his navy bag and pulled out a small plastic pocket from which he drew out his identity card and the hospital papers.

"You can ask them," he said, "sure they'll say I was there."

"We know what we have to do," said Perrault.

But the authenticity of the documents meant there was no doubt. Magnanimously, they let him go, advising him not to dawdle in the area. In any case, he'd had a free lunch.

Then it was the turn of a hitch-hiker, a Dutch student who was wandering about Neuville with his backpack and his guitar. A driver had picked him up at the Beaune exit and had left him three kilometers off, near to a fork in the road. He'd come from the South of France where he'd spent the whole summer and was making his way slowly back to Amsterdam. They asked him where exactly he'd been the week of the 19th to the 26th August. He couldn't quite remember: he'd wandered through Provence, by the Parc du Verdon, and he'd spent the weekend of the 15th August in Draguignan. He was a strapping lad, about six foot, a redhead with long hair.

"Are there any drugs in here?" said Boivin, tapping the large backpack placed on the floor with the tip of his foot.

In an insolent tone, the boy responded that he wasn't stupid enough to travel in a foreign country with hash on him. The idea crossed Boivin's mind to make him completely empty his bag, there and then, to teach him a lesson. But with foreigners, you never know who you're dealing with, and then with the bloody European Union everyone has the right to go all over the place. This one's papers were in order, and he had a credit card.

"Alright," said Perrault, "you can go. You'd do better to get home."

Prudently, the boy held back from telling him where he could put his advice. He continued his journey, without really knowing why they'd stopped him.

After that, the gendarmes didn't know what more they could do. They'd made investigations in the village, they'd spoken to the Jensens' employees, the plumber, Bébert, a vagabond, a hitch-hiker... they couldn't summon just anyone at random.

"We could talk to the Colin boy," Brigadier Boivin proposed, finally, "the one who found the dog."

Having received his summons, François went to the meeting with confidence, supposing they wanted him to recount in detail the circumstances of his discovery. He arrived punctually at eleven-thirty. That day, his work schedule was full. He estimated that the interview would last around half an hour, after which he would have to go and pick up his father, who was ploughing a field, to take him back home. They'd arranged that François would take over on the tractor after lunch. His whole day going to be a busy one.

"Good morning, sir, please sit down."

"Good morning, sirs," said François. Before him were Brigadier Perrault, whom he knew a little since he'd taken part in the search, and the young gendarme in front of his typewriter. When he'd arrived, Brigadier Chief Gallard was also present, but he left the office at the beginning of the interview.

He was made to state his name and show his papers, and the typewriter began to crackle. François, who was not familiar with this kind of place - he hadn't even done his military service as he was suffering from asthma at the time of conscription - was struck by the cold formality of his welcome, the way in which the gendarmes acted as though they didn't know him, when he'd spoken to them several times and had come in good faith in order to help them.

Perrault made him start his story from the beginning, interrupting him at each stage with useless questions: what time exactly did they leave the house, at what moment exactly had they discovered the dog, was it before or after their sandwiches, was it he or his father who'd seen the animal first, had they moved it -

"Of course we didn't move it," said François. "We came straight away to the gendarmerie. We spoke to Brigadier Boivin."

"You said before that you went home first of all."

"Just to put down our bags and the guns. And to tell Mother. Dad wanted to go and see you straight away."

"So you didn't want to, mate?"

"Are we "mates"? As for me, it was just a dead dog, you don't disturb the gendarmes for a dead dog. You see, I didn't know about the missing girl."

"The girl's got a name. She's called Martine Jensen. Don't tell me you don't know the Jensens?"

"I've heard of them, but I never paid much attention."

"They're beautiful girls though.. You don't look at girls?"

"We're not in the same area. Don't have the opportunity to see them much."

"Even so, a man of your age, thirty-five, not married, living with his parents, doesn't seem very normal to me..."

François felt the blood rush to his face.

"What are you trying to say?"

"A red-blooded man of your years has needs..."

"I didn't come there to talk about that," cried out François, furious. He looked at the clock and thought of his father, "I gotta call my mother so she goes and gets Dad, he's working in the field. I should've gone to get him for lunch. We gonna be here much longer?"

Perrault motioned towards the telephone.

"Go ahead. It could be a long one."

And the questions continued. Indecent questions, indiscreet questions, that didn't have anything to do with the subject in hand. Of course, there were questions about the dog, always the same ones, that popped up during the interrogation without rhyme or reason, as if to surprise François, and to which he had to give the same response. This lasted until one o'clock. François hadn't swallowed a morsel since six in the morning and was starting to feel hungry. He asked if they could bring him something to eat, he had the money to pay for it.

"All in good time," said Perrault, "we're not in a hurry. Shall I have something, maybe?"

At two o'clock, Sylviane Colin came to the gendarmerie, demanding to see her son. Request denied, she shouted that he had to work in the field that afternoon, and if he didn't go then his old man would be forced to do it, and that she didn't know what François was doing there, it was shameful to keep people like that without any reason. They told her not to worry, and that if there was really no reason, she'd get her son back soon. She only had to let the gendarmes do their job. Gaston had advised his wife to take a sandwich for François. The gendarmes took it, promising to deliver it to its intended destination.

Seeing the sandwich arrive, prepared by François' mother and wrapped in a red-checked cloth from the farm, Perrault felt tempted to leave it in full view on the desk, under the boy's nose, and to continue the interrogation. But he was hungry, too. In a gesture of compassion, he held out the sandwich to François and left the room.

They left him to eat under the watch of the young gendarme. Then Brigadier Boivin came back.

"You can go," he said to his typewriting colleague, "you've got half an hour."

He sat at the desk in Perrault's place.

"Let's start again!"

"Sunday 15th September," François began, having recuperated a little, "was the start of the hunting season. My father and I left the house at quarter to six, with our two Brittany spaniels, Bandit and Boy. We'd taken our guns with us, and our satchels. In Dad's, Mother had put a sandwich, with raw ham, goat's cheese and a bottle of white wine..."

"Don't be slick, boy" interrupted Boivin, his tone familiar and brusque.

"I dunno what the hell I'm doing here," said François.

"You are being held for questioning under a preliminary investigation."

"And if I don't want to answer?"

"That's for you to see," said Boivin, at once evasive and menacing.

"I'm not saying anything more."

"We could always interrogate your father."

"Let the old man alone," said François.

There was a moment of silence. Boivin reread the notes of the statement that had already been typed.

"So why's that," he began again, "you're not interested in girls?"

"None of your business."

"But it's true... you're not married, not known to have a girlfriend, nothing on the side..."

"Who told you that?"

"We know what there is to know."

"You don't know anything. I have everything I need in Orléans."

"Orléans isn't very close... to have go so far to get some, you wouldn't be a homo, would you?" Since François remained silent, "bear in mind that it would be better for you. It's rare that a homo takes it out on a woman. Although it's been known."

"What do you want from me in all this?" said François, clenching his fists.

"What's bothering us, you see, is that Martine Jensen left without telling her family. It's been a month since they've had any news from her. It's so unlike her, that her sister is asking herself if she isn't already dead."

"If she's been killed, then it's really unfortunate. But it doesn't mean that it happened around here."

"The week after she disappeared," replied Boivin, "we checked all the hospitals and morgues. There was no-one corresponding to her description. And they haven't called us since."

"What can I do about it," said François.

"Tell me what you were doing on the 21st August," Boivin barked at him.

"I was probably working. End of August, we harvested the corn. And we had lots of other things to do. There's work in the fields, in the summer, I don't know if you knew."

"Lose that tone," bellowed Boivin, "you are starting to get up my nose."

He began to bombard François with insidious and absurd questions, questions that François was incapable of answering. How could he find a convincing line of argument about something he was there for over nothing, an affair he knew nothing about? He felt trapped, cornered by bad faith and stupidity, and felt a powerful anger grip him.

Returning from his lunch break, the young gendarme took up his place in front of the typewriter, and inserted a blank page.

"I can't make head or tail of your questions," said François, watching the young gendarme. "I'm not signing anything."

"We'll see about that!" Boivin threatened - knowing very well that he couldn't force him, he didn't even have the right to keep him against his will under a preliminary investigation (but knew that François didn't know that).

"You don't have the right to hound me like this."

"What do you mean, we don't have the right," exclaimed Boivin, "you're a suspect!"

"Suspect for what? There's no reason..."

"Yes there is," returned the gendarme, "you knew where the dog was!"

François jumped up from his seat,

"I didn't know anything! We came across it by chance! Where are you going with this?"

"... from there to thinking that you know where the girl is."

François, who had participated in the searches and had even helped lead them with his father, thanks to their knowledge of the forest, had a fit of rage. Beside himself, he took hold of his chair and lifted it above his head. It looked like he was about to throw it.

"Threatening an officer!" shouted Boivin, triumphantly, "you're a witness, eh, Roland," he added, addressing his young colleague. "Go on, shove him in the hole."

Six o'clock chimed at the Vaucerf farm. Having waited for her son the whole afternoon, Sylviane put the beans that she'd just shelled in to soak, and took off her apron.

"I'm going to look for him."

"It won't help," said Gaston, who was in the middle of reading the news by the light of the window, "it's better you stay here."

"But why are they after him? What do they want from him?"

"Don't worry Mother, they're floundering. They can't do anything to him."

"It makes me feel sick knowing he's over there all alone. They might keep him the whole night, no food, nothing."

Gaston put down his paper and started to refill his pipe.

"It won't kill him."

With a determined step, Sylviane went over to the coat pegs and reached out for her jacket.

"Since you don't give a crap, I'm going!"

"Listen, Mother..."

"Agh, stop calling me Mother, shit, you're twelve years older than me!"

"Calm down then," Gaston continued without becoming flustered. "If you go, they'll chuck you out the minute you set foot in the door."

"My little François," whimpered Sylviane, coming back to sit at the table.

"Your boy, you always molly-coddled him too much."

"He was more sensitive than the others."

"Yeeeessss..." said Gaston, who had his own thoughts on the matter.

"I don't know what to do anymore. My little François..." she repeated.

"Wait until tomorrow," said Gaston. "I'll go, if necessary. And come on, while we're waiting, pour us a drop. That'll lift our spirits."

The next morning at eight o'clock, coming in for his shift, Brigadier Chief Gallard noticed the Colin boy stretched out along the bench in the cell.
"What the hell is he still here for?" he said.
And François was able to go home.

CHAPTER 5.

André pushed open the door to the cafeteria of the CHU Lariboisière hospital where Bruno, who worked sixty hours a week and hardly left the place, had arranged to meet him. He stopped at the entrance, seeking out his ex-brother-in-law in the crowded dining space. He didn't have to look for long: coming up behind him, Bruno tapped him on the shoulder. They took their places in the self-service queue. Plate, cutlery, bread roll... André felt like a student again. He followed Bruno's lead, inwardly smiling; he even found the steam escaping from the kitchen and the heavy smell of the canteen pleasant.

His host directed him to a table that was set apart beside an entire wall of glass panes looking out onto a courtyard decorated with scrawny shrubs.

"Okay for you here?"

"Perfectly," said André.

André began by congratulating Bruno on his work, his stupefying surgical operations which had been discussed in the newspapers, even though the whole idea of fingers, hands and indeed grafted arms sent shivers down his spine.

"It's all team-work" Bruno responded mechanically, which, even so, didn't stop him dreaming of becoming Head of Surgery and of being, one day, the 'Boss'.

André found that Bruno had matured. With his white coat, in the mundane surroundings of a hospital canteen, he didn't seem like such a snob - proud and touchy, inviting celebrities to Boyrive, or joylessly attending family events organised by Paula at Saint-Dominique road. Maybe he was one of these men who only felt at ease in their professional environment, where they knew they were really appreciated. Since Bruno'd begun to prove himself, that must have given him some reassurance... André wondered if he had remarried, though he supposed not. Bruno now seemed totally absorbed by his research and his career. He imagined that he would be more likely to live with his mother, the formidable Madame Dutilleux (who was remorseless towards others, but prostrate before her adored progeny) whom André had met on a few occasions.

"So, it seems that my ex-wife is giving you some cause for concern? Her sister called me two or three weeks ago."

"Yes, you're aware of it. Right now it's been more than a month since we've had any news, and Martione's phone isn't picking up messages any more. I'm worried it might have been destroyed. It's the 23rd September today? That's it, exactly one month and two days."

"Oh," responded Bruno with a little knowing smile, "if I were you, I wouldn't worry too much, Martine is unpredictable."

"Unfortunately we have a new reason to worry. Hunters found her dog in the forest. The police veterinary services concluded that it had been strangled. Judging from the state it was found in, it had been there a while."

"You're sure it was hers? Since it had been there for a while..."

"The police had my wife identify it, who clearly recognised it. It was definitely César, Martine's Labrador, no doubt about it."

"Tell me what I can do to help."

"The last person to have seen Martine was Sammy Moore. Paula went and saw him, she's already spoken to him."

"I know. Sammy called me the next day. He was surprised."

"What's worrying my wife and I is the drug issue. Martine had got out of the habit; she took a bit of coke from time to time - I was almost going to say like everyone does - but nothing to be worried about. And then we found out that she'd recently taken up with this singer and said to ourselves that maybe there was a link. It's only an assumption, you understand, we're looking at everything... so, the day that Martine had Sammy over to Boyrive - which is also the day she disappeared, I'll remind you, from which date no-one had heard from her or seen her - we thought that maybe she'd taken something that didn't agree with her. And we were wondering if someone who'd kicked the habit a while ago could, without knowing it, accidentally take an overdose - a dose that they could have tolerated before, without realising that after a few years of abstinence, the same quantity could kill them... first of all, I wanted to ask your opinion on that."

"It's possible, actually. It could happen."

"Okay, and it's still an assumption, right - but imagine that Martine had an accident that afternoon, when they were both in the bedroom -"

"André, I'm stopping you there. Sammy isn't the little boy he was a few years ago. He's really become someone in his profession, he's got commitments, a team, responsibilities. It would really surprise me if he still took drugs. Especially right now when he's preparing a show to tour throughout France, and at the same time his new album which should come out in December. Surely there are draconian clauses in his contract: recording companies don't kid around these days. And Sammy's has really invested a lot in him, there's a lot of money at stake."

Bruno stopped himself to raise his eyes to a woman who brushed past their table. André saw her from the back as she pushed her shoulders back, and swayed her hips. When she'd passed, Bruno looked at André with a meaningful twinkle in his eye, as if to tell him that he'd already had her.

"Precisely," continued André, without rising to the bait, "if it so happened that one of their star singers had gotten caught up in something, it would be interesting to know just how far the producers would go to get him out of it."

"I don't follow."

"We can only imagine what they would be capable of in order to sort things out, to hush things up, you see?"

Bruno couldn't see; he waited, fork in the air.

"Okay, in a case such as this, it would be in the interests of the recording company to arrange things so that the public doesn't get wind of the affair. It would be understandable, after all, if there was a lot of money at stake..."

"Be more precise," said Bruno, who was starting to get it.

"If Martine had died from an overdose when in the company of her singer, the producers could have done whatever was necessary to make the body disappear, there, that's what I wanted to say."

"No," said Bruno, "impossible."

"Concealing an accident is not committing a murder."

"No," said Bruno, "they wouldn't get mixed up in something to the point of hiding a body. I don't believe that at all. A recording company would never do that."

He went back to eating. He'd got a meal fit for an athlete: salad, spaghetti, cheese and fruit - which he swallowed methodically, without either distaste or pleasure, as if he were putting fuel into a machine.

"Everything depends on who exactly has interests in the business," responded André, following through on his idea, "and just whose money keeps it ticking over."

Bruno's expression was incredulous, disgusted. Evidently, Doctor Dutilleux lived in a world far removed from these kinds of sordid affairs...

"Sammy's recording company is a vintage one, a respectable one," he said, "They're not angels of course, but to go from that to... No, what they'd probably do to support one of their stars in trouble is to send him their lawyers."

"Most vintage labels have been bought up by immense corporations," replied André, "and dirty money is spreading everywhere right now, everywhere there's a juicy profit to be had. It's there where you suspect it least, believe me. And it's spreading further and further."

"The Mafia, now?!" exclaimed Bruno, "okay, now it's like we're in a bad film."

André pulled back a little.

"It's just a suggestion."

"Have you told the police about your sister-in-law's disappearance?"

"The Neuville gendarmes were informed the very first day. They're looking into it, at least since the dog was discovered, but they've got no evidence and don't know which end to approach the problem from. That's why I'm trying to help them, to find a lead... I was able to get a meeting for Paula with one of the Directors of the Judicial Police. He advised her to leave it to the gendarmes for the moment. The judicial police are waiting for them to find something. As far as they're concerned, as long as they haven't found a body, my wife's sister is on holiday, and that's it."

"And what do you think?" asked Bruno, noting the defeated expression of his interlocutor.

"I'm pessimistic."

"How's Paula doing?"

"She's very down, especially since she identified the dog. She hardly goes out of the apartment any more. It's hard, what's happened to her... I'm trying to leave her alone as little as possible, but I've got a business to run and there's no question of me leaving it right now. I call her several times a day."

Bruno was thoughtful. He remembered the beautiful, loving and vivacious young woman he'd known, whose body was possibly right now decomposing in the undergrowth.

"You've got to ask yourself why these kinds of things happen," he said flatly.

In his heart of hearts, he didn't give a damn. At the beginning of the summer, when he'd last seen her - at her request, simply because she was bored in that hole at Boyrive - and he'd taken her out of sheer politeness firstly to Deauville and then to some other party, when he'd realised that they didn't have anything else to say to each other. As beautiful as she was - and she had seemed possibly even more so now than when he'd known her before - he didn't want her anymore. In reality, their marriage had been a mistake. You marry a young woman thinking you'll be able to mould her how you want, a young woman from a good family moreover - a banker for a father, even the fussy Madame Dutilleux had approved of the marriage - and you find yourself with a chatty, insolent airhead, with personal opinions about everything, who thinks she's an artist...

He suggested, out of politeness,

"Would you like me to talk to Sammy, to ask him to think harder, try and remember any details he might have forgotten?" (Although in reality he had no intention of getting involved in an affair that would only create distance between him and an amusing and famous friend). "As for the recording company," he said again, "I'm sorry, but I've no way of knowing who finances it, and I believe that Sammy doesn't either, he won't have even asked himself the question... but now I think about it, maybe Paula has kept in contact with some of her father's friends. A bank could easily help her find out something like that."

"It'll have to be the police who ask that. And the police can't do anything. You could put Martine's bloody dress under their noses but, without a body, they wouldn't move... or very little."

"You paint a black picture there."

"Hardly - that's just how it works."

Bruno looked at his watch and then at the cafeteria clock.

"Believe me when I say I'm sorry, I wish I might have been able to help you... but anyway," he said, "nothing's certain and Martine might end up getting in contact."

"Let's hope so."

"Please excuse me, but I have to get back, I've got a meeting in ten minutes." He got up, "I'm going to get a coffee, you want one?"

Sammy Moore walked last night's companion to his apartment door. She asked him for some money for a taxi. Knowing exactly what this innocent request signified, Sammy placed two hundred euros, which he had set aside earlier, into her hand. She thanked him with a kiss on the cheek.

"You'll call me?"

"Yeah, yeah," he said, gently pushing her out.

"You've got a letter," she pointed out to him, indicating the envelope that stuck out of the doormat.

'All whores,' he said to himself, smiling, when he'd closed the door. But he preferred the groupies (who were at heart just poor kids, hardly any different to the girls he hung out with ten years ago in Grenoble) to call girls, with their model poses, their affectation of good manners and their semblance of education.

The envelope that he'd just picked up carried the stamp of the Neuville Gendarmerie. He unfolded the letter and read it, unsurprised: a summons. Since Paula Jensen had come to see him on Ponthieu Road while he was rehearsing, he had waited to be questioned as a witness, given that he was the last known person to have seen her sister. He'd even thought that it would have happened earlier and had started to hope that Martine had resurfaced. He read the summons a second time. They wanted to see him Friday 27th, in two days' time.

He put the letter in his pocket and set about walking through his apartment, three hundred and fifty meters squared on the desirable Boulevard de Courcelles, a bourgeois apartment that his agent had found for him and that he'd bought fully furnished from an American actress with money advanced by the recording company - bloody stupid. The luxury that had flattered and amused him at first was beginning to get him down. When, clad in Hermes mules given by an admirer, he wandered about on the cream woolen fitted carpet, in the midst of varnished furniture and padded sofas, he could have taken himself for the famous period actor Sacha Guitry. His mates laughed at him (which didn't stop them raiding his bar, though). For a while now, he'd been dreaming of moving to an area that suited him a little better. And he'd have to get rid of the Ferrari as well; nothing but trouble, that car! Sammy went into the bathroom. His musicians were expecting him at ten o'clock, there was no time to lose.

On the way to the studio, thinking it prudent to take some legal counsel before going to see the police, he called his solicitor and made an appointment for that evening. Until then, apart from Bruno who'd been linked to the family and already knew what was happening, he hadn't spoken about Martine's disappearance to anyone. Not to his agent, not to the recording company, and especially not to his mates. No use spicing up idle chatter that would surely reach the ears of the paparazzi, who were never very far away.

In any case, he had nothing to reproach himself about. That fateful day, he had left his companion in great shape and in an excellent mood. She'd accompanied him to the property gate while he drove slowly by her side, and when they were about to separate, she'd kissed him again. He didn't know where the relationship would lead to, but he liked Martine Jensen. She was a woman with class, the exact opposite of the girls he usually hung out with, the groupies, or those who were just starting out in show-biz and were only thinking of their careers.

And then soon after he'd heard nothing from her. The following Monday, he'd tried in vain to get hold of her on her mobile, and then two days later her sister came to interrogate him in the recording studio. He had nothing to do with Martine's disappearance but that wasn't enough to reassure him. If the story got out, and if it was known that he'd been questioned by the gendarmes, he saw only too well what the media would do with it, since he was such a success: the news scoop on the TV, the juicy articles with his photo in the regional and national press! And he thought also of his parents who ran a bakery in the suburbs of Grenoble, of their shame on discovering, from the front page of the Dauphiné Libéré, that their son had been involved in such a sordid affair. His father and mother, so proud of him, who had become sort of stars themselves in their district since he'd given a concert in the town he'd been born in...

More seriously, supposing that Martine had been murdered, and that they find her body in the vicinity of Boyrive, he could only imagine the problems he'd have with the gendarmes if they didn't have any other suspect on hand. His career over, a possible miscarriage of justice, prison... and wait, what if they'd found the body and it was for that reason that they'd called him in? At this thought, Sammy felt a twinge of terror. For a moment he contemplated calling Paula Jensen, who probably knew what the gendarmes were up to, then dropped the idea.

After a day in the studio, Sammy put on a clean shirt and went directly to his solicitor's - who, not having a single moment free during the day, had made an appointment for him at eight o'clock that night. It was preferable, in any case, as the singer wasn't then in any danger of seeing anyone else there and being recognised.

Mr Bataille opened the door himself. He was a man in his sixties, an experienced solicitor who had already helpfully advised him regarding a disagreement with his producers. He was a corporate lawyer, but Sammy didn't know anyone else. And this one frequently dealt with artists: he understood the problems that celebrities found themselves facing. Sammy followed him to his office through the deserted corridors of the company offices. Mr Bataille received visitors in a little holed-up room; the padded door and a thick oriental carpet that almost entirely covered the floor blocked out almost all noise; the files were hidden away, locked up in a large mahogany cupboard. As it was the end of the day, two lamps had been lit which gave off a warm and intimate light. It was a setting reminiscent of the novels of Balzac, it encouraged the sharing of confidences and respect for secrets. After having invited his client to sit down, Mr Bataille set himself down behind his desk.

"Well, Sammy, what wind blew you in?"

By way of reply, Sammy held out the gendarmes' summons. The solicitor rapidly read through it and placed it back down within reach.

"Yes?" he said.

Whilst his visitor recounted his story, the solicitor observed him attentively. Like most of his fellow lawyers, Mr Bataille was not overly trusting. When someone in trouble came to him to explain an affair, his first impulse was to ask himself if they were leading him up the garden path. Having argued in his defence against his producers, who wanted him to sign an unconscionable contract, he knew Sammy a little. His opinion of him was of an intelligent and stubborn boy, a hidden character - at that very moment, even though he had come of his own accord to ask for help, he avoided making eye contact - certainly he was devious, despite his dimples and the disarming smile. You don't get to where Sammy was at the age of thirty - and stay there - without a singular adroitness.

"This kind of thing is a real nuisance," he said with a concerned air when the singer had finished speaking, "you never know where it's going to lead, you could find yourself weighed under with complications."

Sammy paled.

"It's just that," continued the solicitor, "underlying every judicial error, there is often a certain clumsiness on the part of the accused - a lie, an omission, a fact that he'd thought wise to hide and that, once discovered, irrevocably casts suspicion on him and can have terrible consequences. The files are filled with such cases."

"But I haven't lied to you, I've lied to no-one" Sammy protested, "when I saw Martine Jensen the last time, she was really well, and she was in a really good mood. What else can I tell you?"

"You didn't argue... fight, perhaps?"

"I've never raised my hand to a woman," Sammy protested.

"You didn't consume anything that day that could have made her ill?"

"All we had was two glasses of Chevalier-Montrachet," (Mr Bataille mentally clicked his tongue - with such a wine, really, there is no need for coke to look on the bright side of life, and he stopped himself from asking about its vintage just in time) "I went to choose the bottle with Martine," Sammy explained, "they had an excellent cellar in Boyrive. If it's drugs you're thinking about, I can reassure you on that straight away: let me say it again now: I've touched nothing for the last three months."

"Not even a little cocaine? Cocaine's very stimulating."

"Not a gram. There's a clause about it in my contract."

"Okay. You were telling me you'd left your companion at five pm. You arrived at five-past seven at your meeting in Fouquet's..."

"I saw lots of people, too."

"Perfect. In the intervening time, that period of two hours, did anyone see you?"

"I stopped on the motorway to fill up. It must have been around half five."

"You paid by credit card?"

"No, with cash. But the pump attendant recognised me. He called over his colleague and I signed an autograph for them. They'll remember me."

"That could be useful at some point. But it doesn't tell us what state you left your friend in."

"I'm telling you, she was fine. She went with me to the gate."

"I believe you (and he was, in fact, starting to believe him), but it has to be proved."

"What are the gendarmes going to ask me? What should I tell them?"

"The truth. Above all, don't hide anything from them. Stick to the hard and fast truth."

"In their letter, they don't even say if they've found Martine (for once, Sammy's gaze was fixed on the solicitor, a look filled with anxiety), I was thinking of calling her sister. She's got to know at what point they're at. If they've found the body, they must have told the family."

"Don't do anything, for goodness' sake. The Gendarmerie hasn't yet opened an official investigation, which means they don't have anything." He picked up the summons lying on the desk, "It's only a preliminary enquiry, it states that clearly." The solicitor let out a little laugh, "You're lucky that you're well-known, they're taking precautions! They're not always so open with everyone else."

Sammy looked at him, not understanding.

"A preliminary investigation," explained the solicitor, "is a sort of investigation during which the gendarmes can't question you without your consent. You could perfectly well refuse to go."

"Really?" said Sammy, calmer, "so I don't have to go?"

"On the contrary, I advise you to go. Demonstrate that you're cooperating, you only want to help them, that you went all that way to see them despite the huge amount of work you have, because you're worried about your friend. You are worried about your friend, aren't you?" the solicitor demanded brusquely.

Sammy appeared abashed.

"...well yes, of course."

"Go alone, with a car of a common make, no use in drawing attention to yourself. Be natural and unaffected. Don't try and charm them, the gendarmes are cleverer than they look. Whatever they say to you, stay calm and in control of yourself (but on that point, the solicitor wasn't worried about Sammy). And show some interest in their investigation but not too much of course..."

"God no, this must be some kind of nightmare" the singer interrupted him, "these kind of recommendations are unbelievable! Listening to you, you'd think I was guilty!"

"Let's be prepared in advance. Up until now, they haven't found this young woman's body. But it could happen. So don't forget that you were the last one to have seen her alive."

Two days later, coming out of the Gendarmerie, Sammy remarked to himself that the interview hadn't been too bad. Following his solicitor's advice, he'd gone to Neuville with a rental car, a Renault Laguna, not too flashy or too modest, in casual attire that was also appropriate: moccasins, jeans, and a suede jacket. The questioning was led by the Brigadier Chief. Sammy made an effort to give accurate responses without seeming impatient, even when the questions became rather personal and embarrassing or he had to answer the same ones again and again. A few times, like the good actor he was, Sammy lifted his eyes to him with a clear gaze full of sincerity, avoiding using his usual melting little-boy look. On the whole, the gendarmes were polite, almost friendly. At the end, they'd thanked him for his statement and got him to sign some of his records that they'd bought for their children.

Something bothered him, though. He got back into his car, drove to the motorway and parked in the first parking space he came to in order to call Mr Bataille.

"Well?" the solicitor asked, his tone eager.

"It went quite well. but there's a problem: they found Martine's dog, strangled."

"There, you see!" exclaimed the solicitor as if the news had given him some satisfaction, we were right to be prudent... where was the dog? Near her house?"

"I don't know exactly. In the forest, I think. That could mean that Martine's not far off?"

"That's what we should be worried about."

"But if they find her, they'll also find the murderer?"

"Let's hope. There's always a chance."

"What are the odds?" Sammy asked quickly.

"It depends. Statistically, let's say fifty-fifty."

"Not more?"

"And it'll probably take time. Evidently, it would be better for you if they don't find your friend."

Mr Bataille detected Sammy's distress on the other end of the phone.

"Come on, don't worry about it," he concluded with a calming voice, "If things continue, come back to see me. I don't deal with criminal law, but I can send you to a colleague who's a specialist. He's very good."

Sammy snapped off his mobile, white as a sheet, and threw himself on the steering wheel in childish abandon. He didn't, however, have an emotional temperament: after a few seconds he pulled himself up, mechanically searching for his cigarettes in his jacket pockets before remembering that he'd also stopped smoking. No alcohol, no coke, no cigarettes for months... everything was forbidden because of his fucking job! An ascetic existence. For a while now, he'd even dropped his group of mates to go out with a fantastic girl, a girl with real class who gave him a sense of peace - which was entirely new for him - and the impression of having gained access to a privileged and protected world. And here he was, implicated in an appalling affair because of her, a criminal affair that was maybe going to send his career up in smoke! He turned the key in the ignition and revved up the engine, furious.

That first day of October, it was raining in Paris. Through the living room window, Paula watched it fall on the Jacques Bainville square and beyond that, on the Boulevard Saint-Germain, which was bathed in a grey light, almost wintry. It was late morning, and she'd just woken up for the third time. Her nights were filled with nightmares, punctuated with long hours of restless wakefulness. The night before, she'd had a particularly disturbing nightmare: instead of César, Martine was lying in the veterinary service room at the police station like her dog, half-devoured and her entrails spilling out; she was talking, but Paula couldn't understand what she was saying. In another nightmare, which she'd had several times, her sister reappeared in Boyrive, in a sort of shimmering game of mirages, and Paula, who knew she was dead but believed that she'd been resuscitated, tried in vain to hold her. Or Paula dreamt that she herself was struggling in the foaming waters of a river in flood, with one of her arms cut off: she endeavoured to stay afloat, thrashing her stump desperately. Her nightmares woke her with a start and, strangely for those of her dreams that recurred, always at the same moment. They played with the logic of a horror film and occasionally, when she'd managed to get back to sleep, her nightmares would start again exactly where she'd left them.

Her mouth thick and furry, she went into the kitchen to get a glass of water. The maid looked sadly at the breakfast plate that she'd just picked up from her employer's bedroom.

"Madame, you haven't eaten anything. Monsieur is going to tell me off, he wants me to get you to eat. What would you like for lunch?"

"Whatever you want."

In the last month, Paula had lost 13 pounds; she didn't go out any more and seemed to no longer be interested in anything.

"And, please excuse me, but it would do you good to go shopping. In autumn, you usually renew your wardrobe."

André had said the same thing to her that morning. Go shopping, pick out some clothes, she'd done it a dozen times with Martine. They'd start by checking out the Bon Marché store, and would then go on to the boutiques on the Sèvres road and Grenelle street. Sometimes, they'd cross over the river Seine and scour Montaigne Avenue, or the celebrated Faubourg Saint-Honoré from one end to the other. They'd advise each other, squabble, have salad for lunch with a glass of champagne, set off again to try on some items, having as much fun as a couple of crazies: two sisters who loved each other, who had only each other in the whole world.

Paula looked outside: it was still miserable but it wasn't raining hard, and suddenly she wanted to feel the freshness of drops of rain on her skin.

"You're right," she said, "I'm going out. To walk around a bit. You can make me an omelette if you like."

She had a shower, slipped on her trousers, a jumper and good shoes. Swallowing down her omelette - the maid had traitorously added potatoes and cheese - she went back into the lounge and dialed the number for Boyrive. Having made it known throughout Neuville that if anyone should remember the smallest detail about her sister they could call her on that number, she checked the Boyrive answerphone several times a day. Until then, she'd only gotten two messages, both uttered by the same drunken voice, breathing heavily, as though the speaker was frightening himself: "Your slut of a sister got what she deserved," and "it'll soon be your turn", enriched with lewd details. She had, however, been expecting this kind of thing, and it was such a caricature that it didn't really do much to her.

But this time, to her great surprise, she found a message from the day before addressed to Martine, a mundane message such as living people usually receive, and which sent her brutally back several weeks: the Neuville dry-cleaner reminded her sister that her suits and her linen were ready. Paula picked up her raincoat, went down the stairs four at a time and ran to her car.

The residents of Neuville had two laundromat-dry-cleaners at their disposal: one in the centre, in the Town Hall square, and the other on the outskirts, next to the supermarket - it was this last one that Martine had chosen since she found it convenient to drop off her clothes when she went to do the shopping. When Paula arrived, the owner's face lit up.

"Ah, hello Madame Jensen. I'm just finishing with this customer and I'll be with you in a moment."

Paula, who was going into the dry-cleaners for the first time, realised that she thought she was Martine, and once again felt a shock as if suddenly this case of mistaken identity had brought Martine back to life.

The owner finished with her client and turned to Paula.

"I didn't know what to do, your things have been here a while... I wanted to let you know before shutting for the holidays and then it just went out of my mind. So please excuse me what with getting ready to go, the children, the suitcases, when you're doing all that you don't know where to turn! Do you have your receipt?"

"No," said Paula, "I'm not your customer, I'm just her sister."

"Ah, well you look just like each other, you two, especially with your blond hair, I mixed you both up... Did she give you her receipt?"

"It's been lost," said Paula, "you've surely got a copy, though?" she added, remembering the message she'd left, "there's some suits and some linen."

The owner looked in her receipt book.

"There it is!" she said, "She was supposed to pick it up the 29th August, the Thursday, you see... she must have forgotten, or maybe she went on holiday as well?"

"When did she leave them?"

"Usually a week beforehand."

"Thursday 22nd, then?" said Paula.

"No, not the Thursday. That's the Laundromat's day, the van comes by on Thursday morning very early. She must have dropped them off earlier. Oh, hang on, now I remember, she'd brought them to me the day before, in the evening, I was about to pull down the shutter - on Wednesdays, I close earlier because of the children... that's it, I'm sure of it now, she came by on Wednesday at six o'clock, five minutes later and she would've missed it."

The owner went off and came back with a packet of linen that she put down on the counter.

"I've just re-opened, we opened up again on Saturday," she explained, bustling about, "that's why I didn't telephone before. This year I went on holiday in September, so the shop was closed from the 6th to the 28th. I take it in turns with my colleague down on the square, one goes off in August, and the other in September, that way there's always a dry-cleaners open." She picked up three suits, "so I can give them to you without the receipt?" On principal, she was hesitating, but on the other hand she didn't want to be landed with the clothes and linen.

"I can sign a receipt for you," suggested Paula, pulling out a hundred-euro note from her bag.

"Oh, no need, Madame Jensen..."

Paula put the packets in the boot and sat beside the wheel again. She knew then that on Wednesday, at six o'clock in the evening, her sister was still alive, and seemed to be quite fine. Sammy Moore had said he'd gone that same day to his appointment at Fouquet's at seven o'clock. If he'd told the truth, he'd have no trouble proving it and that would leave him in the clear: taking into account the heavy traffic at the end of the day in the capital, even with his racing car, he couldn't possibly have covered the distance between Boyrive and Paris, and got as far as the Champs-Elysées, in sixty minutes. He must therefore have left Martine at least half an hour before she went, alive and well, to the dry-cleaner's - which the owner will testify to. But even if the singer was out of the picture, Paula herself was no further forward.

For a moment, she thought about going to The Old Oak, then changed her mind, put off immediately by the thought of facing the curious looks, the commiseration, the whispering; she even feared Yvette's concern for her, her displays of powerlessness. And she worried about bothering her: when in trouble, there comes a time when one's presence is just embarrassing for other people.

She preferred to go to the Gendarmerie, even though she didn't hope for much. Ringing the doorbell of the small building, she felt apprehensive, worried about a lukewarm reception, or just not being welcome at all. In such a case where the crime hadn't been established, where there were only assumptions made on the basis of the discovery of a dog, they had already done a lot and to no avail. Paula could see that they were weary of it. She herself didn't have many more resources, she felt empty, at the end of her tether.

"I would like to see Brigadier Gallard," she said into the speakerphone, in a timid voice that was unusual for her.

Against all expectations, she was greeted with a satisfied "Ah!" followed by a fuss in the background, and finally, click, the door was opened. Upon entering, the atmosphere was friendly, they were looking at her warmly, with smiling eyes.

"Please follow me, Madame," a gendarme told her amiably, "the Brigadier Chief will see you straight away."

Gallard welcomed her with open arms, took her hand to shake it, and kept it in his while he led her to a seat.

"I was just about to telephone you," he said with enthusiasm. "We have some good news."

Paula sat in front of him, on her guard, not daring to hope.

"So," the gendarme began, "it seems that your sister has used her credit card. We have proof of it being used in Rouen and Le Havre."

"When was that?"

"The end of August," he consulted his paper, "Thursday 22nd. In the morning, she used it in Rouen three times, and a few hours later in Le Havre - Le Havre," he repeated dreamily, "the Port of Havre..."

"Nothing proves it was her," said Paula, "maybe her card was stolen. What was it used for?"

"Well, that's actually the most interesting part. The card was used for payment in a pharmacy, a leather-wares store and a clothes store!"

"You're sure that it's hers?"

"Absolutely. See for yourself," he said, holding out the paper.

Paula recognised her sister's name and that of her bank, but she couldn't quite believe what her eyes were seeing. She memorised the names of the three stores, promising herself to verify if they were mentioned in Martine's card statement that detailed her activity between the 1st and 31st August, and had probably arrived at the house in Boyrive as it did every month. She gave the paper back to the Brigadier Chief without saying a word.

"Then," he said, "the same day, with the same card, she took out money from the ATM in Le Havre, the maximum authorised amount. We therefore have every reason to believe that your sister is still alive," he declared, with an optimistic smile.

Paula was overwhelmed.

"She wouldn't have done that to me!" she thought out loud.

The Brigadier contented himself with nodding his head while smiling, with the air of one who had seen many such cases.

"...and her dog? She also just left her dog?"

"There are, unfortunately, many abandoned dogs. This one must have had a bad run in with a prowler, someone with bad intentions."

"No," said Paula, "Martine would never have abandoned César. I don't believe it. Okay, it's her credit card, but there's nothing to prove that it's her who used it."

"It's for that very reason that I wanted to talk to you. We need some good pictures of your sister, recent photos. I will send them to our colleagues in Rouen who have agreed to help out: they will go and show them to the retailers in question. There's a good chance that they'll recognise her, if I remember rightly, your sister was very striking-looking."

"If they've seen her," said Paula, still incredulous, "When do you need the photos by?"

"The sooner the better."

Paula got up, thinking she would probably find some in her sister's apartment.

"I'll bring them to you by this evening."

Brigadier Gallard accompanied her to the office door.

"See you soon," said Paula, "and, uh, thanks." On the verge of crossing the threshold, she thought better of it, not unhappy to also have something to tell them, "I nearly forgot, I just went to Martine's dry-cleaner. The owner's certain she saw her in the cleaners at six o'clock the evening she disappeared.

"Ah, great!" said Gallard, closing the door on her.

He waited five minutes until his visitor had gone and then reopened the door.

"Tell me," he said to no-one in particular, "the singer, Sammy Moore, what time did he say he arrived in Paris on the evening in question?"

"Seven o'clock, chief," responded Boivin. "And as he said, he was at the petrol station on the motorway around half-five. It's a definite, the pump attendant remembers because he asked for his autograph. As for the day, he can't remember exactly, but they're certain about the time because one of them was on night shift and had just arrived."

"You've already checked it out?" Gallard remarked with surprise.

"Well, yes! They're talented, these arty types are, they think they can manipulate the whole world - but they mustn't take us for pea-brains. Just because we let him go doesn't mean we don't keep an eye on him." He emphasised with a large laugh.

Gallard went back into his office, suppressing the desire to rub his hands: decidedly, it had been a good day. To start with, at this stage of the enquiry everything pointed to the idea that, whatever had happened to Martine Jensen, it hadn't happened in Neuville, and that therefore he probably wouldn't have a murder case on his hands. In any case, since the missing woman had been seen in Neuville after the departure of the singer, he no longer had to deal with the unpleasant prospect of re-questioning him (and pressing him further this time too): and what's more, detaining a show-biz star... Brigadier Chief Gallard was fifteen months from retirement and hoped to switch to managing the motor vehicle fleet of the Departmental Council. He had already started preparing the ground and, thanks to his excellent performance (in his sector, the percentage of resolved cases had been 60% the preceding year) he had a good chance of being given the desired position. It wasn't a good time to damage his success rate.

Two Brigadiers from the Rouen Gendarmerie departmental company came out of the Old Market Pharmacy, one carried an envelope of photos under his arm. Since the beginning of the morning, they had conscientiously been carrying out the mission conferred to them by their Neuville colleagues.

In the pharmacy, a resounding negative. Too many clients came through the store for the employees to remember a person's face. It was the same thing at the leather retailers, which they had been to just beforehand: the shop assistant was new, brought in on the 1st

September, and couldn't therefore help them regarding any clients who'd come in August. The third store they'd been asked to visit was the fashion boutique, 'Amandine', situated opposite the pharmacy on the other side of the market: they only had to walk through the square to get to it.

The arrival of the gendarmes in Amandine caused a sensation. Customers and shop assistants stopped what they were doing, turning towards them with stupefied expressions. The store manager walked forward to meet them, her heavy bust so far thrust forward it made them wonder whether it was to welcome them or push them out. When they explained their business to her, the manager ushered them out of view of the customers and took them into the back room. Without wasting any time, they spread out the photos on the table. Paula, who didn't know what her sister was wearing the day she disappeared, had chosen three which showed her in different lights: the first was a portrait, her hair up, her features clearly distinguishable, the other two were full-length, Martine's hair down and floaty. In one she was in jeans, in the other she was in a summer dress.

"I've never seen this person," said the manager, having examined the photos. "But I'm not always in the shop, I have to do the accounts and the stock-taking."

They brought in a shop assistant, who said that the photos vaguely reminded her of someone, nothing more, she couldn't say anything for certain. If this person had been in, in any case, she hadn't served her.

"Send in Anne-Marie," the manager ordered.

To the relief of the gendarmes, Anne-Marie immediately recognised her customer.

"Yes, I remember this lady very well. I sold her some lingerie. She was tall and slim, but with a bust too - her bra was a 34D. She bought quite a lot of stuff, I don't usually sell so much in one go... Afterwards, she wanted some clothes and it was Catherine who took over."

Called in her turn, the third assistant confirmed what her colleague had said.

"She wanted some trousers. She bought two off me, with jumpers, shirts and a jacket. She quickly packed it all away in a big linen bag. I thought she was going on a trip."

"So, gentlemen, do you have what you need?" asked the manager, eager to finish and not wishing to leave the counters unmanned.

Neglecting to question the fourth and last sales assistant, since two of them had already recognised the woman they were searching for, the gendarmes thanked her and packed away their photos.

"I told you that that woman was weird," whispered Catherine to her mate at the lingerie counter when they went back into the boutique.

"You were right, and she also made a strange impression on me. She didn't even try anything on, as if it was all the same to her what she was buying."

"Well that's great, eh, these women who have money, give themselves airs and graces... and then, actually, they have the police running after them."

The manager reappeared, accompanying her visitors to the door. The assistants went quiet and took their places. Happy with the success of their investigation, the Normandy gendarmes left at a brisk pace to telephone their colleagues in the Ile-de-France with the good news.

CHAPTER 6.

There are times in our lives when we experience unalloyed happiness and which seemingly mark the apogee of life's journey. For André's father the postwar years had been just such a period: the beginning of those glorious years of reconstruction when effort bore fruit, where he had built-up his construction company and started a family, years he always looked back to with nostalgia. But, in equal measure, there are those moments where everything seems to come crashing down around you. After several peaceful years during which André's life had been an easy journey along a well-marked road, all at once his sister-in-law had been kidnapped, his wife brought to the brink of depression, and he, one so used to being in control of every situation, suddenly found himself a plaything in the hands of the mafia.

It was nearly seven-thirty. All of André's employees had left and, in the silence of his office in La

Garenne, with the lights switched off leaving him in a crepuscular semi-darkness, André pondered the events of the preceding months from the day when, after the 'incidents' for which his merchandise had paid the price, M. Rouleau had been persuaded by his new friends from Moscow to resume his exports under their supervision.

In the beginning, everything had gone smoothly. The cosmetics manufacturer had nothing but praise for their services: his merchandise arrived at their intended destinations safe and sound, and the recipients made their payments regularly, only too happy to see a very lucrative business pick up again. Of course, he had to give a portion of the money to his protectors, destined - so they said - to pay off the police officers who kept an eye on the shipments (the poor devils were so badly paid...). But since the Russians' help translated into substantial gains for him, then rather than see it as an extortion payment Monsieur Rouleau preferred to consider the large cash-in-hand sums as a sort of commission.

For André, it was extremely beneficial: a guarantee of regular business, no more stolen vans or kidnapped drivers. There were even some exhilarating moments.

The first time, while they were loading the boxes of lipstick onto one of the lorries, André spotted a grey Mercedes parked on the road in front of the courtyard. When the lorry started up, the car followed it at a respectable distance, matching its speed to the lorry's.

One month later, they were preparing the second shipment. The Mercedes was in position. It was cold that day and André, consumed by curiosity, went up to the car to say hello and to offer the driver some coffee. Four huge blokes sat wedged into the seats, with expressions that were far from friendly. They all responded to his 'Bonjour!' with a brief nod of the head. As for the coffee, it was a curt "Niet... spasiba.... niet, niet." Their hand gestures said it all - they weren't there to make friends.

Once the lorry had left with its escort, André turned to his client, "with guys like that, I definitely feel looked after..." which made them laugh, like the two imbeciles that they were.

And, as they'd promised, Mr **Yakovlev** and Mr **Loukachenko** weren't long in sending some clients André's way, although he was never able to meet them. André dealt instead with a freight forwarder, a sort of intermediary who monitored the transportation of the freight from a distance and took care of the formalities, travelling by plane and flying stopovers from one destination to another.

He was a giant with a huge face and the almond eyes of Mongolia; a Russian who spoke a sort of pidgin French (and five other languages) without any articles (which the Russian language lacks of course) and without any conjugations either. He went by the musical name of Evgueni. With thirty words of business French, he nevertheless managed to make himself understood: "Me guarantee ten transport contracts for year," he said to André when they first met, in a sonorous baritone and furiously rolling his 'r's', "VasseurTransEurope no worry searching merchandise, merchandise arrive warehouse with documents all order. VasseurTransEurope do only transshipping and dispatch." Curiously, Evgueni had never asked to visit the warehouse, nor to see the equipment, as though he had already been assured of the capability of his carrier. To seal the deal, he promised "Me do everything possible assure return cargo." This final point sealed André's agreement, as he never liked to see his lorries return empty. He discussed his prices and made up a preliminary quote, which the man accepted without a murmur. They agreed that VasseurTransEurope would be paid by bank transfer to the company account.

André quickly noticed, however, that the merchandise that was conferred to him had taken bizarre routes. Spanish and Portuguese lorries soon landed on his warehouse doorstep, as did vans from Eastern Europe and the Baltic states. The merchandise that he then had to transfer into his own lorries was packed into locked and bolted containers, or was in hermetically sealed bundles. Not even the most astute could have made out the containers'contents. The return trajectories were no less surprising. Departing from Moscow, his driver went to deliver bottles of detergent to Tallin or Helsinki. The bottles were replaced by furniture or by Scandinavian crockery that was taken to Germany. In Berlin, the load was dropped off in its turn and substituted for cases of canned beer. Then back to La Garenne-Colombes where, again, a new load was picked up. Under Evgueni's attentive gaze, the beer was transferred to another lorry and replaced with toys headed for Spain; or with bundles of handicrafts that had come from Africa via the Portuguese coast, to be sent to the Cote d'Azur. The empty lorry was quickly filled with tomato sauce and packets of pasta before returning to La Garenne, where a container marked 'sports shoes' was added to its cargo, a change of driver and off it went, en route for Moscow. As André's lorry drivers jokingly said, this was "return cargo with a twist."

As it happened, the lorry drivers loved the detours, especially the driver most often sent to the East, whom the Russians, with their legendary generosity, welcomed like a king and sent back home to France with a fur chapka or an astrakhan hat, gifted moreover with a bottle of vodka or a box of caviar. Once, just before Christmas, he'd even been given a fur coat for his wife... "My otchin lioublim franzim!" the Russians shouted merrily at him as they escorted him back to his lorry the moment he had to be off on the road again.

For sure, they adored France, this crossroads of international trucking traffic, this kind country of transit where one lorry in three was foreign and the border controls didn't know where to put themselves any more... "Ya lioubliou russiya otchen otchen... da svidaniïa... see you soon!" the driver would call back to them, as he was now able to garble a few words of their language.

After the second journey, André realised that they were getting him to transport black-market and counterfeit goods. The flasks of 'detergent' delivered to Finland and Estonia were actually bottles of gin, vodka or whisky that, under this innocent name, escaped the heavy taxes levied on alcohol. The lorries coming from Lisbon, reputed to transport 'authentic African handicrafts' were actually taking, via a complicated circuitous route over land and sea, copies of Louis Vuitton bags, counterfeit Hermès scarves, shirts embroidered with a fake crocodile - actually made in Indonesia or in China. The cans of beer loaded in Berlin were great for hiding so-called big-brand watches, all the way from Moscow and destined for the Spanish, along with low-cost cigarettes peddled on the French markets, mobile phones flogged on Italian beaches, and so on. The outlandish itineraries and the multiple loadings and unloadings were enough to cover their tracks by masking the real origin of the counterfeit products, which would otherwise have aroused the suspicions of the customs guards.

André began to worry. But how could he get out of it? He'd been commissioned by Evgueni to undertake ten journeys, and in business you don't easily retract what you've signed up for, especially with this kind of client. André couldn't even think about speaking to customs: he would have gotten himself killed in retaliation, and maybe one of his drivers too. Instead he decided to wait and see. Given the incredible density of cargo traffic, the chances of one of his lorries getting caught were slim. The papers that the drivers presented at the control posts - doubles of order receipts, customs declarations, export slips - were more real than the real ones. In the beginning, even André had been taken in by them. And it was probable that, at certain border posts, the customs officials were corrupt or had been threatened.

As if to confirm his suspicions, the payments made to VasseurTransEurope were made by bank transfer from various tax havens: Nassau, Gibraltar, the Cayman Islands... André could very well have said that his 'clients' thought he was an idiot and he could have asked them for a lot more money but, on reflection, he'd judged it preferable to be paid at a reasonable rate, which avoided compromising him and allowed him, if need be, to pretend not to have realised what they were getting him to transport. Finally, he had decided that the best thing would be to undertake the contracted ten journeys. His contract fulfilled, he would find an excuse not to renew it.

But it wasn't long before things got complicated. One morning, the Mercedes that usually served as an escort to M. Rouleau's expeditions pulled into the courtyard. Evgueni got out of it with an amiable smile and holding in his hands a wooden casket that was nailed and held shut by a metal band. Evgueni wanted him to send it with one of his regular loads to Milan, but it had to be done discretely, without any paperwork. He was asking him as a favour.

André wanted to know what was inside.

"Nitchivo... just some parts for computer games. Present for school for small children."

"Impossible!" André replied. "If the lorry was checked.... the package would need documentation. And where would you have me put it?"

"Small corner of lorry," Evgueni suggested, "Small parcel..."

At a glance, the box measured 15 centimetres square. André wondered what might really be inside. Perhaps it contained illicit copies of precious hi-tech materials, microchips, data sticks or - worse - precious items like smuggled diamonds...

"No," he said, "too dangerous. If a customs official lands on me, what'll I tell him?"

"No borders in Europe," Evgueni replied, "border controls finish!"

"It's even worse," André replied, "they can stop my lorries anywhere, you're no longer safe from checks at all - No," he repeated, "it's too risky. And how do I know what this box contains?"

The smile vanished from Evgueni's face. Six-foot-three inches tall, and 270 pounds, he looked him up and down, his narrow, bright eyes bearing down on him, clearly saying: the less you know, the better.

In the courtyard, departing from their normal way of doing things, the passengers from the Mercedes had climbed out of the car and were smoking cigarettes as they looked over in their direction with a threatening insistence. Suddenly, André was afraid; for himself, for his family, for his staff. He asked:

"And how will it get picked up?"

"Driver drops box to Milan apartment. I give address."

It just kept getting better: now he had to take one of his drivers into his confidence.

"I don't know if I'll find anyone," said André, "perhaps they won't agree."

"Just one time," said Evgueni, resuming his easy-going manner, "One small time. Nice present for driver."

André agreed, feeling like man who was digging his own grave. He changed his team's rota, causing a ruckus among the drivers who were switched around at the last minute, and chose one of the older ones, one of the guys who had worked for him since the creation of the business and on whose discretion he knew he could rely.

Luckily, having been transported underneath the sleeping berth, the box arrived at its destination without any trouble.

A few weeks passed before one morning (it was near the end of May), the Mercedes pulled into the courtyard again. This time Evgueni got out empty-handed. With a serious air, he announced to André that he had to speak to him about an important matter and asked him, in his very persuasive way, to organise a rendez-vous in a quiet location.

Five days later, on Monday the 3rd June, having found nowhere that was quieter or more isolated than the family property at Boyrive, André found himself in the office of Paula's father, accompanied by Evgueni and a man named Igor, a sort of bodyguard cum henchman, a sinister-looking man whom André had already seen at the wheel of the Mercedes as he escorted the lorries.

Evgueni's project involved transporting 100 kilos of cocaine, in two loads, in the Vasseur lorries. Nothing less than that - these people didn't do things by half... The biggest payload, at ninety kilos, had to go to Bialystok, in Poland, near the border with Belarus, and the remaining ten kilos to Milan, the same address where, a few weeks earlier, André had to get one of his drivers to deliver a box with undisclosed contents. This time, however, they were open about the nature of the cargo: it was 95% pure Bolivian cocaine, and worth more than four million euros!

Evgueni placed an overnight bag down on the desk containing the 10 kilos destined for Milan, which André was supposed to slip into one of his containers carrying a normal cargo load. He had also brought a briefcase which he opened hurriedly, containing 225 000 euros stacked up in rows of 100 euro bills. This bonanza represented half of André's compensation, it being understood that the other half would be paid to him once the two loads had been transported and all the merchandise had reached its destination. Almost a quarter of a million euros in cash! Evgueni appeared very self-satisfied. He seemed encouraging and rather proud of the proposal, certain that no-one could resist such a generous offer.

André was astounded. He felt like he was in some kind of nightmare, or playing a role in a bad movie. He had never for a second imagined getting involved in such a serious criminal enterprise, of becoming an accomplice in the poisoning of thousands of people, all the while risking a heavy jail term. And he had no desire for this money which - something that a man like Evgueni couldn't understand - didn't mean anything more to him than a great big bloody disaster: an extra trinket for Paula, who didn't really attach any great importance to such things, a new car for himself, but he changed the car every two years anyway at the business' expense. A nice holiday... and then?

He remained quiet.

Evgueni, in a tone that was at once engaging and reassuring, all the while underlining what he was saying with dramatic gestures to compensate for his insufficient vocabulary, then listed the possible hiding places for the ninety kilos, which made up the largest part of the cargo: a false floor and a false ceiling in the truck, hubcaps, stuffing the seats, the bumper... but André didn't have to worry about that, he wouldn't have to do anything: a team who were well practiced in this kind of work, watched over by Igor here, would come to the warehouse at night with the merchandise and would prepare the lorry...

Dumbfounded, his ears ringing, André wondered how he could get himself out of this mess; to buy some time, he'd asked to see the contents of the briefcase and Evgueni, though reticently, had lifted the lid to reveal ten one-kilo-bags of cocaine pressed one against the other like packets of flour, next to the case full to the brim with money.

André remembered having uttered something bizarre, the first thing that came to mind: "... and the sniffer dogs?" when suddenly the study door opened, revealing the charming face of his sister-in-law who exclaimed "oh, sorry!" before quickly shutting it again.

The whole thing hadn't lasted more than three seconds, but the colossal, oh-so-recognisable slav had met the intruder's eye. "My wife's sister," André had explained, embarrassed, "I didn't know she was there." Disappointed and furious, Evgueni left there and then with his bodyguard and cases.

Although relieved to see them depart, with their dirty money and their dangerous crap, André was worried about what he was going to say to his sister-in-law. He quickly went into the kitchen where he'd found her, relaxed and smiling, in the middle of making some coffee. "Do you want a cup? Forgive me for barging in earlier, I didn't know you were there. I'm really sorry..." "No worry," André had replied.

Martine told him that she'd set herself up at the house in Boyrive two days previously, and she'd just come back from walking César along the Essonne. Coming in through the kitchen door, at the back of the house, she hadn't seen the parked cars in the courtyard. As she walked through the main hall to go up the stairs and take the first floor corridor that led to her apartment, she'd heard the murmur of voices in the study and had gone to check it out.

But it had been so fast, and she'd been so confused to have disturbed them, that she'd closed the door too quickly to have noticed anything in particular - just her brother-in-law having a meeting with two people.

André said that he'd been near to the house with two new clients and, instead of taking them all the way back to La Garenne, he'd thought it would be simpler to take them there to talk, which all three had agreed upon. Martine kindly reminded him that it was also his home and that he didn't have anything to explain to her.

And the whole thing had stopped there. If Martine had said anything to her sister, which wasn't certain, Paula, with her usual discretion, didn't think it worth talking to her husband about. Perish the thought that they conduct an investigation into their own family!

André's thoughts were interrupted by the ring of his mobile phone.

"You okay?" his wife asked him, "I'm not disturbing you?"

"No. And you, how're you?"

"Okay, I'm at the house. I haven't moved all day. Where're you?"

"At La Garenne, there's no-one else here now, everyone's gone. You wanted to tell me something?"

"Two sales assistants in a shop in Rouen recognised Martine's photo. Brigadier Gallard just called me."

"Oh fantastic, that's good news!" said André.

"I don't know."

"Oh come on, it is..."

"But what's she gone to do all alone in Rouen?"

"Maybe she's not alone."

"What're you doing tonight? You coming home for dinner?"

"I've got to go by **Balzac** road first, I've got a quote to go over. But, if you like, I'll reserve a table at Fouquet's... get dolled up, I'll meet you there in two hours."

"I don't know."

"Come on darling, push yourself a little... do it for me."

"If you want... okay, okay, I'll see you there."

When Paula arrived at the restaurant, the ground-floor room was packed. As she hesitated on the threshold, looking for her husband, all eyes converged on her. André, who was seated at a table facing the door, felt proud. His wife was wearing a black Jersey dress with long sleeves and a high collar, enhanced with a flowing bias drape from the corset, and carried a velvet jacket on her arm. Her hair was simply pulled back into a chignon, but she had done her make-up with care. In her high-heeled court shoes, which gave her an extra ten centimeters, she had the imposing stature of a model; and yet one could also sense a touching fragility, certainly due to the ordeal she was undergoing.

André got up to pull out a chair for her and brushed her cheek with a light kiss.

"You are so beautiful tonight... very elegant."

"Thank you," said Paula as she sat down.

"You decided to go shopping then... that's a new dress?"

"It was one of Mum's dresses. I just had the hem brought down."

"You don't see many dresses like that any more," said André, "proper, well cut womanly dresses... you want an aperitif?"

"If you do. A Martini."

André ordered for them and looked at his wife. He was happy that she'd made an effort to get dressed, a good sign that she was trying to get back on track.

"How're you? You're looking better."

"Humph," Paula muttered, "and you, you had a good day?"

"The usual."

"Have the problems you told me about been resolved?"

"Yes, don't worry," André lied through his teeth, "it's resolved, everything's okay. So the Gendarme in Neuville called? What did he say?"

"What I told you: two girls saw Martine in Rouen Thursday 22nd, which was the day before she stood me up. They recognised her immediately. He seemed very pleased with himself, Gallard, I swear he was almost triumphant... he had the tone of someone who's proclaiming good news."

"Well, it is for him. It's a huge weight off his shoulders."

"That's what I thought as well. He doesn't care what happened to my sister as long as it's not in his district."

"There's someone else who'll be relieved too," said André, "and that's the singer, Sammy Moore... did you tell Sammy the news?"

"No," said Paula, "I didn't even think about it."

"Put yourself in his shoes..."

"Well, yes. I don't really want to call him, the gendarmes will do it, I suppose."

"We've caused him a lot of trouble, all the same. He must be worried sick."

"Ah, maybe. I should call him, then?"

André stayed quiet. He was always surprised by his wife's indifference, her tranquil upper-class womanly selfishness.

"Leave it," he said finally. "I'll call Bruno. He'll be only too happy to tell Sammy, and be the bearer of good news."

Paula contemplated the brightly-lit room; the immaculate tablecloths, the sparkling glasses and silver cutlery, the bustling to-ings and fro-ings, the greetings of those just arriving passing from table to table (half of the people present worked in cinema and knew each other more or less), the loud bursts of laughter...

"It's busy tonight."

"It's autumn, everyone's back from their holidays."

"They seem so busy, so happy," said Paula sadly.

"Don't believe it, they've all got their share of worries and suffering, their work, money, health problems either for themselves or a loved one, loneliness... it's just they try and overcome it. You mustn't let yourself be overcome by adversity, you understand, darling, you must fight..." saying these brave words, André didn't really know if he was speaking to his wife or if he was boosting himself with the encouragement.

"Yes," said Paula, in a little voice, "precisely..."

The wine steward arrived, and announced "Chablis-Vaudésir 1996," uncorked the bottle, and poured out a little into André's glass.

"That's fine, thank you," said André having tasted it.

The glasses half-filled, the wine steward gave way to the waiter who had brought a pyramid of langoustines.

"Precisely," Paula said again when they had left, "I wanted to talk to you about something."

"Mmm?" said André, attacking the shellfish on his plate.

"I was saying to myself, now they think Martine's left - in fact, since some money was taken out at Le Havre with her card, they're convinced that she's boarded a boat - the gendarmes will stop looking for her..."

"Probably."

"So I thought about getting in a private detective."

André's langoustine tail nearly went down the wrong way. A private detective! That's all he needed right now! Someone who'd come rummaging through his warehouses, sniffing at the lorries and chatting with the chauffeurs - and who one day would come across the picturesque freight forwarder, Evgueni...

"What do you think?"

"It's an idea... I'll have to see."

"See what?" said Paula.

André thought quickly.

"The type of detective, the trustworthiness of that sort of person... you don't want to get just anyone in, you'd have to have someone who's serious - you want me to handle it?" he proposed, telling himself that, detective for detective, it would be better if he were his own personal client.

"Oh no, I can't lumber you with that. This afternoon I called an old friend of my father's, one of his colleagues at the bank. He gave me an address..."

"You told him what it's about? A detective who works for a bank isn't necessarily someone who's any good at finding missing people."

"It's an agency that the bank employs. The best in Paris, or so I'm told. It seems they get great results. They'll send me to someone who has the right profile."

André wiped his lips slowly and swallowed three long gulps of Chablis in one.

"Well, well, well," he said, letting out a deep sigh, "do as you like."

The first interview Paula had with the detective that the directors of the RBI agency (Renaud Brossard Investigations) had presented to her lasted two hours. Although the agency took up a whole floor of a plush building on the sought-after Boulevard Haussmann, she was welcomed into a relatively modest office that looked out onto a courtyard. The detective apologised for his office, saying that he wasn't often there. Paula liked him straight away. A little filled-out gentleman with salt-and-pepper hair, he must have been around fifty. Two dreamy blue eyes lit up his calm face, which was slightly rounded and he talked with a calm, controlled voice. With his gentle appearance and serious air, he could have been taken for the director of a small provincial post office. His service record, however, was impressive. He was called Henri Berger, a name that wasn't totally unknown to Paula, who remembered having heard him being discussed a while ago in connection with an affair that had caused a right hullabaloo: the owners of a palace in Biarritz and of several small hotels on the Basque coast, whose daughter had disappeared, presumed kidnapped or maybe murdered, had made the police's lives a misery with no result. Hired as a last resort, Henri Berger only took a month to find the daughter: under an assumed name, she was working as a demonstrator of household automated convenience devices in a department store in Dayton, Ohio. Pushed to the limit by the zealous authoritarianism of her parents and by their perpetual use of money as blackmail, this rich kid had fled, on the eve of her eighteenth birthday, practically without a penny in her pocket. Whilst admiring her determination, and although really she was now an adult, the detective believed he was still obliged to betray her: she was still, after all, very young.

Throughout the whole interview, Henri Berger managed to get Paula to talk even without asking many questions. She understood that he needed information and he inspired confidence in her. For the first time since her sister had disappeared, she had the impression that here was someone who was really listening.

The detective left for Rouen the next day. Arriving in the center of town at ten past five, he parked near to the Old Market Square and walked over to the Amandine boutique. A glance through the shop window confirmed the presence of the sales assistants that his client had talked about. Guessing that he'd be thrown out by the boutique's manager if he tried to distract them during working hours, he noted the closing time, intending to come back and question the young women when they left.

That gave him one and a half hours. He went around the businesses that were set on the square with the photos of Martine Jensen that her sister had given him. He started with the pharmacy and the leather shop where they knew the young woman had used her Visa card - without much more success than the Rouen gendarmes. Then, he visited the two hairdressers, the perfume shop, the newsagents, even the bakers', standing discreetly beside the sales counter until the sales assistants had finished with their clients and could really pay attention to him. Henri Berger was a methodical and patient man who wasn't put off by this thankless door-to-door travelling salesmanship: throughout his career, he had gathered many precious bits of information through this humble medium. He finished by going to the cafés, restaurants and the three nearest hotels, all without success. The hotel receptionists, sitting bored behind their desks, consented to open up their registers: the name Martine Jensen wasn't registered for the 21st August, and not for the following days either. At five to seven, having rewarded himself with half a pint, he was back in front of the Amandine boutique.

Inside, three young women were slipping on their coats. The light turned off and they came out together. Night was falling. Henri approached them, taking care to remain at a respectful distance.

"Good evening, Mesdemoiselles..." three small, suspicious faces rose up to look at him. He remembered a name that was mentioned in the gendarmes' report that his client had handed to him, "which one of you is Anne-Marie?"

"What do you want?" asked a small brunette.

"Let me introduce myself," he said, following protocol, "Henri Berger, private detective."

"Private detective!" exclaimed the girls in unison, thrilled (here was a break from the usual routine). "I'm Anne-Marie," the brunette hastened to add, "how do you know my name?"

"I've been tasked with finding a missing person," he said. While talking, he showed them the photos.

"But we know these photos!" cried out Anne-Marie, "we've already seen them... It's the woman that the gendarmes were looking for when they came by the shop last week! We recognised her straight away, she'd come to the shop near the end of August... right, Catherine?"

"Yeah, she'd bought some clothes, like for a boat."

"For a boat?" repeated the detective.

"Sports clothes, a navy sweater, a sailor's jacket, all that. We thought she was going to take a boat trip."

"And also loads of lingerie... What did she do?"

"She didn't do anything wrong. Her elder sister is looking for her, that's all. We don't know what's become of her.

"Oh, that's why she seemed so strange."

"What do you mean, strange?"

"She wasn't like someone who's buying clothes. She wasn't smiling, she wasn't joking. You could say she was in a mood."

"It was more that she seemed sad, I'd say. So they still haven't found her?"

"Unfortunately not. That's why I've come to see you. I thought you could help us one more time."

"Ah, but we already told the gendarmes everything!"

"I was wondering what time she came to the shop: was it the morning or the evening?"

"In the morning!" Anne-Marie and Catherine responded together.

"Was she alone?"

"Ah no, I don't think so. When she arrived, she was with a man... but he went out straight away."

"He went out?"

"Yes," said the third young woman, who hadn't said anything yet, "the men often do that. They come in with their girlfriend and after five minutes they go out and wait for them in the street... as if they're ashamed to be there!"

The young women all burst out laughing.

"Could you describe him to me, the man who was with her, tell me what he looked like?"

"Nothing special," said Catherine, "he wasn't very tall, brown hair..."

"More like chestnut brown hair" Anne-Marie corrected her.

"Brown. And he wore a grey suit."

"His suit was blue with stripes."

"A blue or a grey suit?" questioned the detective, smiling.

"Okay, I can't remember all that well," said Catherine, "Gotta go now, my parents are waiting for me."

"It's Cécile you should ask," suggested the third girl, "her station is at the counter next to the window. She can see everything that goes on outside."

"And she's not there today, your colleague Cécile?"

"She's had a day off for her grandfather's funeral. But she'll be back tomorrow, you can ask her then."

"Go on then, I don't want to keep you much longer," finished the detective, "thank you very much, Mesdemoiselles. Until tomorrow then. What time do you get out for lunch?"

"The boutique's closed from half twelve to three o'clock."

Happy provincials, he thought as he walked back to his car. Not the kind to grab a quick bite to eat for lunch. He booked a room at the Le Havre Mercury Hotel and decided to get himself a sea-food platter in the pretty beach village of Sainte-Adresse.

He was already at the port by eight o'clock the next day, wandering along the Vauban docks. It was sunny and fresh. He breathed in deep lungfuls of invigorating sea air whilst admiring the boats, freight ships for the most part. It didn't escape Henri Berger's notice that there were no more liners at the Le Havre docks, just the mixed freight ships that, along with their cargo, also took passengers on certain dates. He started by questioning the men who worked on the quays. With them, no need for preliminaries: all he had to do was to say hello and put the photos under their noses. The dockers, however, after occasionally letting out an appreciative whistle, shook their heads to indicate no. He went around all the wharfs without forgetting the docking station for ferries that went back and forth to and from England. The task took him two hours, after which he hopped back into his car and drove north to the marina, made up of two bays that were entirely filled with private vessels. Unfortunately, as it was autumn, it was starting to get cold and the owners were nowhere to be found. Looking at the hundreds of moored boats, yachts, chris-crafts, small boats and speedboats covered with tarpaulin and sailboats with rolled-up sails, the detective realised the magnitude of his task if he had to find and question each of the owners who'd been there at the end of August - a superhuman feat.

He walked to the end of the north harbour pier which, along with the tip of the south pier, formed the mouth of the harbour. Out here he was buffeted by the wind from offshore as it blew vigorously. Henri Berger held his face up to it, scrutinising the agitated surface of the sea, listening to the sound of the waves as they hit the rocks of the harbour jetty at regular intervals, as if they tirelessly beat out a message that was his task to decipher. He stayed there a good while. For the first time since the beginning of the investigation, he felt a sensation that he knew all too well, a wave of quite vibrant emotion, an interior shock that served as an alarm that he was exactly where he needed to be.

He consulted his watch and retraced his steps. He still had to drive the ninety kilometers from Le Havre to Rouen. He didn't have any more time to waste if he wanted to be there when his new friends, the little sales assistants of the Amandine, came out at half twelve.

This time, Cécile was there. He offered to buy all four of them a soda on the terrace of the Café Flaubert. This time, they felt at ease, they chattered and laughed, excited by a situation that gave them some importance: participating in an inquiry, collaborating with a detective... they would talk about it for a long time between themselves, and would attentively follow the affair if it happened to be mentioned in the news.

Cécile seemed a bit older than her young colleagues - Henri thought her twenty-five, thirty maybe - and she gave the impression of being someone reasonable and credible. She stated she remembered perfectly well this man who was pacing up and down the pavement while the woman he'd accompanied was choosing her clothes; as she didn't have anyone to serve at that moment, she had been at leisure to observe him. According to her, he was a man of about forty, rich brown hair but with pale skin, almost grey. He was wearing an old-fashioned double-breasted suit, too heavy for the season. She had also remarked that he was wearing thick black glasses even though it was cloudy that morning. He didn't look like someone from Rouen: she thought he wasn't even French, but it was only an impression, she couldn't confirm it. Anyway, the man seemed different somehow, he'd intrigued her, and that's why she remembered him so well.

Henri, who'd noted in a book everything that Cécile was saying as she spoke, asked the young women why they hadn't said anything about Martine Jensen's companion to the gendarmes.

"Because they didn't ask!" they responded with one voice.

"I wasn't even shown the photos," Cécile said, who'd felt quite hurt.

Henri Berger understood that the Rouen gendarmes, happy with their two positive eye-witnesses, had left again, content to leave it at that.

Paula saw the detective's car come through the gate that she'd intentionally left open and went into the courtyard to welcome him. She held out her hand to him: he had a firm and brief handshake.

"Beautiful house," he said, walking around with an admiring look.

"Thank you. It's a family home. It was passed down from our grand-parents."

She took him to the study, showed him a seat and sat opposite him in the place she'd seen so often occupied by her father. The detective placed his leather briefcase at his feet and waited. She invited him to speak with a smile.

"I've just come from Rouen," he said, "I got back last night. I have news."

Thinking it was needless to alarm his client prematurely by giving her his own impressions, which were not great, he limited himself to reporting the statements of the Amandine employees, keeping strictly to the facts.

"When your sister went to the boutique in Rouen, she wasn't alone. The sales assistants noticed that a man was accompanying her."

"Do you think these girls are trustworthy? They didn't invent it to make themselves interesting?"

"No, I believe them. Their statements tally. It rang true."

"What did this guy look like?"

"A brown-haired man, around forty, medium build."

"You're telling me my sister ran off with someone?"

"I said she wasn't alone, that's all."

Paula fixed her gaze on him for a moment in silence.

"Okay, it's curious," she said, "but the owner of the café in Neuville called me this morning to say that one of her customers claims he saw a man driving my sister's car."

"When?"

"The day she disappeared. Near here, near Boyrive."

"Could I talk to this customer?"

"Of course. But first you want to see Martine's apartment, I believe?"

Henri Berger acquiesced.

"I'll take you through."

But she didn't move to get up. She hesitated, still on her guard, as though surprised at entrusting this much to someone whom she didn't even know a week ago.

"Tell me, Monsieur Berger," she asked, "are you married?"

"I was. My wife left me. You know, with my work schedule, the impromptu travel, it was hard for her..." he let out a brief laugh, "she married a taxman - a stable man. She always knows where he is, what time he's coming home..."

"You have kids?"

"Two. A girl and a boy. But they're big now, they're adults."

"My sister's also an adult. I'm only older than her by two years and yet - I shouldn't say it - I've always considered her a little like my own child, even before our parent's death. She was a small, temperamental girl, imaginative... exactly the opposite of me, and she was fragile too, very early on I felt that I needed to protect her. I don't want to seem too solemn, but right now I feel obliged to find her, or at the very least to find out what happened to her. For her, for myself, for my father and mother... you're going to do the impossible, aren't you?"

She finally got up, and invited him to follow her. They crossed the courtyard and Paula opened the studio for him. She hadn't gone in for many weeks; it was just too painful.

"She did her paintings here. She'd studied fine art. She could have been an artist, I don't know. We weren't very concerned with all things artsy in our family. Martine was the first..." Paula attacked the stairs, "her bedroom is on the first floor, I'll show you."

The detective noted that she'd talked about her sister in the past tense and he said to himself that, maybe unconsciously, she was losing hope.

Having run his gaze over the room he glanced at the bathroom. He pulled out a screwdriver with multiple heads from his briefcase.

"What are you going to do with that?" said Paula, startled.

"Sometimes you find papers slid behind a bathroom cupboard, a sink tile, underneath a fixed item of furniture... precisely the things we want to hide and which could be important: a telephone number, a name, an address... I'll put everything back, of course." Since Paula didn't look like she was going to move, he added, "these systematic searches, are, well, indiscreet. I'm going to have to explore the pockets of her clothes, turn out her handbags, her cases..."

Paula went to the huge wall closet and slid back a door with an energetic gesture.

"Go ahead," she said, revealing the hundred dresses and suits that were enclosed within.

"She had a computer," noted the detective.

"Turn it on if you want, but she never used it. She wasn't even connected to the Internet. You won't find any emails. You think it'll take you long?"

"Including the ground floor, maybe an hour and a half, or two."

"Okay, I'll leave you to work. Close the door when you've finished and come get me in the kitchen. I'll take you to The Old Oak, the café that I told you about. Good luck, and take your time," she said before leaving.

Seeing Paula Jensen coming into the establishment, in the company of a man he didn't know, Bébert nose-dived into his Ricard. He knew that her younger sister had been spotted a long way off from Neuville, somewhere in Normandy, in Rouen if he remembered correctly: the gendarmes, who'd had enough of being considered a bunch of incompetents, had made sure that the news had spread and that the whole region knew about it. But now there was no further risk of them coming and pestering him and the whole village was no longer buzzing, he felt a kind of remorse at continuing to hide what he'd seen. The eldest was still looking for her sister and he suspected, with good reason, that the poor thing was still in torment.

The newcomers were talking at the bar with Yvette; Bébert, who observed them out of the corner of his eye, had the impression that they were scheming about something. When he'd arrived at The Old Oak just an hour earlier, the owner had been particularly friendly and several times, he'd caught her giving him a sideways glance as though to assure herself that he was still there. At one point, confirming his suspicions, Yvette came over.

"You don't need anything, Bébert? You want some more ice?"

"No, it's fine," he said, waving her away.

Yvette sat down authoritatively at the table.

"Listen Bébert, I have to talk to you seriously..."

"Go on then."

She told him that Paula, who didn't believe that her sister had gone off of her own free will, had hired a private detective to find her.

"She's having a hard time, what with losing her younger sister, think about it. She's worried that something bad has happened to her. And if anyone has seen anything out of the ordinary, then, if you ask me, I think it's their duty to talk about it."

"I don't get involved in other people's affairs," said Bébert, who didn't like being lectured.

"I know, and you're right. Me either. But sometimes we have to. Martine Jensen might be in danger. We might still be able to save her, who knows? Sometimes we see things, a small detail that seems like nothing, and that could save someone..."

"What do you want?" said Bébert.

"It's about what you told me. The 308 that you saw when coming back from Nicholas's place, with a guy who was driving it, a guy who wasn't from around here... you know, hey, I didn't talk to the gendarmes about it since you didn't want me to."

Bébert, who thought highly of her for that, agreed with a nod of the head.

"But now they're not dealing with the whole thing anymore, if you wanted to have a word about it with the man over there, he's Madame Jensen's detective, eh, and you know, Bébert, it could be very, very useful."

"Tell them to come over," said Bébert, who'd made her beg long enough.

Yvette returned to the bar, negotiated for a minute with the two others, then Bébert saw Paula Jensen leave the café while the man came over to his table.

"Henri Berger," the man introduced himself, "Private Detective." He touched the back of an empty chair, "May I? I'm going to have a drink," he added, convivially looking at Bébert's glass, "May I get you one too?" On the defensive, Bébert refused with a hand gesture. "I'll have a Ricard," called out the detective to Yvette. And he got straight to the point, "So, it appears you noticed a car on the day that Mademoiselle Jensen disappeared?"

"That's what I said."

"You recognised her own car, a Peugeot 308?"

"That's right."

"And it wasn't Mademoiselle Jensen who was driving?"

"No, it wasn't her."

"There was a man at the wheel?"

"That's right."

Henri Berger asked himself if the brevity of his interlocutor, who was already fairly inebriated, was to stop himself from spluttering or if it was simple peasant wariness. He decided on the latter: despite his bloodshot eyes, and the puffiness of his face, Bébert seemed to know what he was saying. He'd once known someone like that, a man who'd boozed the whole way through his retirement: at the age of eighty, he talked well and walked straight, from his house to the bar, from the bar back to his house, regular as clockwork. Then one day he'd felt under the weather, his doctor had told him to stop drinking, and he'd died one week later.

"So," the detective started again, "it was a man who was driving... do you remember what he was like?"

"He wasn't from around here."

"What did he look like?"

"Oh, eh," said Bébert, who'd had a lot of time to think about what he was going to say, "he had brown hair and black glasses, thick-rimmed sunglasses."

"What was he wearing?"

"I didn't see. I just passed him by, him in the car, me on the bike, it happened quickly."

"Was Martine Jensen sat by him?"

"No, there was no-one else in the front."

"And in the back, was there anyone?"

"I didn't see nothin'."

"What direction was he going in?"

"Towards the motorway."

"And where was he coming from?"

"At the time, I thought he was coming from the Jensen house, which would have been logical seen as it was one of the girls' cars..."

"But you're not sure?"

"There's a bend just there, so I didn't really see him coming out from that stretch. He could have come from higher up, from the forest path..."

"What time was that?"

"A little before eight, I was off for dinner."

"Is there anything else you'd like to tell me?"

"Eh, no, I didn't see anythin' else."

Berger drained his glass and got up.

"Thank you for your statement, you've given us some important information."

Bébert responded with an evasive gesture.

Returning to his car, the detective called his client in Boyrive and shared the results of the interview with her. In his opinion, the man who'd been seen in her sister's car and the man who accompanied her to the boutique in Rouen were probably one and the same person: the descriptions given by Bébert and the Amandine sales assistants tallied. Paula thanked him and encouraged him to keep going. Since he'd taken the investigation in hand, with his patience and knowledge, his experience, and maybe even a sort of sixth sense, she felt that things were progressing and that they were getting closer to the truth.

Even though he hadn't said anything yet, given the lack of hard evidence, there was no doubt in Henri Berger's mind that his client's sister had been kidnapped. In fact, he had been fairly certain of it since their first meeting, when Paula Jensen, who'd been very distressed, had come to see him in his office. Firstly, there was the missed meeting: a discourtesy that was hardly in keeping with well brought-up young ladies who were close to each other. Then there was this silence for several weeks which made him even doubt that Martine Jensen was still alive (it was the 8th October, she had disappeared the 21st August, and so her family hadn't had any news of her for a month and a half).

A voluntary departure was unlikely. The young woman had left her apartment (which he'd minutely combed through without finding the smallest indication of any planned travels - nor, for that matter, the smallest note or telephone number that could have given him a lead) as if she was about to come back at any moment: suitcases and toiletries were all there, bottles left open, the jewellery drawer was full and left half open, the wardrobe full to bursting... not exactly the apartment of someone about to leave for several weeks, or even for a few days.

The fact that the man had been seen on his own in the 308 implied the existence of another car, which Bébert hadn't seen, and in which the young woman had probably been placed. There could, therefore, have been several assailants. One could have grabbed her in the forest while she was coming back from the dry-cleaners, stopping the car to walk the dog - which would have been between about six-fifteen and seven thirty, since Mademoiselle Jensen had gone to the dry-cleaners at six o'clock and Bébert had passed the 308 around quarter to eight. Maybe the driver had strangled the dog, who was bothering them, and rejoined his companions having left the dog on the other side of the woods, a good distance from the property so that it wouldn't be discovered and identified too quickly. Henri Berger told himself that the 308 itself, borrowed for a moment from its owner, would probably have seemed an encumbrance and one of these days it would be found in the Seine when being searched on another occasion, among the dozen bits of flotsam and jetsam thrown there for various reasons: carcases of stolen and stripped-down cars, insurance swindles...

And then, above all, there was this intuitive feeling that he'd had in Le Havre, when he found himself at the end of the North harbour jetty, that Martine Jensen had been there, that she'd boarded at the marina. His intuition would be confirmed for a simple reason: if the kidnappers had boarded a boat, it wouldn't have been a freight ship where they would get noticed and for which they would have had to reserve their tickets far in advance; it was more likely it had been a private boat, a yacht for example, which could have been anchored a little further out and they could have gotten to by rowing boat. Since one of them had been seen at Boyrive early in the evening of the 21st August, and then in Rouen on the morning of the 22nd, they no doubt had a discreet hide-away nearby where they'd spent the night.

The fact remained that the young woman had gone to a fashion boutique, in the centre of town, and to at least two other shops, without alerting anyone or trying to get away. The detective therefore inferred that her kidnappers must have lied to her, to make her believe that they were simply taking her out of the equation for a while and threatened to execute her, her or her sister, if she tried to get away. And maybe that really was their intention at that time, simply to get her away from there and keep her separated from something, then they didn't know what to do with her anymore and the most prudent of them, the most determined, made the decision on behalf of everyone: he had himself eliminated their captive and gotten rid of the body by throwing it into the sea. And the detective told himself that, maybe, this was the message the waves were trying to give him, at the port of Le Havre, when he heard them beating, with regular strokes, the rocks of the harbour...

Martine Jensen had been kidnapped, of that he was certain. The question now was to know by whom and, since there had been no ransom demands, why.

CHAPTER 7.

Henri Berger had only been employed for a week, and he already knew that his client's husband had a mistress. He had made the discovery by chance, while he was looking for a possible lead while wandering around the business's neighbourhood, in La Garenne-Colombes. Until then, he had never met André Vasseur: he had his name and the address of his warehouse from his wife; all the same, André Vasseur only knew the detective by name.

It was then five in the afternoon and Henri Berger was wandering around near the gate of the establishment, taking in the air, waiting for who-knew-what... when suddenly a brand-new car pulled out of the courtyard, a shiny metallic grey BMW 530, sparkling like silver in the sunlight. It had a Paris number plate, and was driven by a middle-aged man, well turned-out, wearing a tie. The detective thought it might be the boss's car and, without having planned to, he followed it.

Driving slowly, the BMW reached Asnières, the neighbouring town, passed through the town centre and headed out north to an outlying area. It had stopped in front of a row of little houses side by side, set back from the street by a tiny patch of front lawn – what looked like a row of council houses. Henri Berger had first thought that André Vasseur was visiting a sick employee; he parked a bit further off, expecting to have to wait for quarter of an hour. Two hours later, night had fallen, and he was still there, standing watch like a rooky police officer. Finally André Vasseur emerged, arm-in-arm with a young woman who accompanied him to his car. She kissed him one last time, and he returned her embrace, tenderly, taking his time: it was clear that this woman meant more to him than just a brief fling.

Then, just when André Vasseur was driving off, a small three or four-year-old boy came running out of the house and threw himself in his mother's arms. The relationship between all three of them seemed so natural, so familiar, that the detective had immediately thought the boy was their son. He allowed the BMW to drive off, contenting himself with noting down the house's street address: 14 Paul-Eluard Street.

The next day, returning to gather more information, a neighbour set him straight. She was a woman of around 50, still wearing her dressing gown at midday: evidently bored to the back teeth, she viewed the detective's visit as a godsend. This type of character is the salvation of those doing research. He hardly needed to question her. Imagining - since a detective was asking questions about her - that her young neighbour ("her at number 14") was in trouble, she spilt the beans on everything she knew, and even about things she didn't know, without waiting to be asked.

"Her at number 14" was a single mum working as a waitress at the Brasserie de la Gare. She dropped off her son at the day care every morning and picked him up again at the end of the school day at half four. At that age, children go to bed early, which allowed her to have all her evenings free to receive whoever she wanted ("If you know what I mean"). The man whom the detective talked about, undoubtedly a married man, came to see her two or three times a week in the late afternoon. From time to time he spent the night, on one occasion he even spent the whole weekend... and this merry-go-round had been going on for several months! Made you wonder what he could be telling his wife...

She'd heard that he was the boss of a lorry transport business in La Garenne or Bois-Colombes, she couldn't remember anymore. But, in her opinion, the guy looked more like a gangster, like in those American action films, Casino or Mafia Blues... his car, a luxury vehicle like he had, looked out of place on Paul-Eluard street; this was a street for decent people, the houses were allocated by the Town Council and not to just anyone. She herself was a widow of a municipal employee, an electrician who'd died in a work accident. It wasn't an area for a kept woman...

"But you told me that she worked," the detective felt prompted to remark.

"A waitress in a bar, hey," the woman replied with a knowing look, "nothing more practical for meeting people. There's the proof..."

In short, it was thanks to the boy that she'd been allocated the house, as they were a single-parent family. The two of them had arrived together two years previously, the little one was very sweet, but no-one knew who the father was - that poor kid... And now she'd found this chap who'd bought her a fur coat, a marmot coat (it's not because she'd never had one that she didn't know what they were). And on top of that, this woman was working! It didn't bother her to steal work from someone who would have really needed it... you can't say, the neighbour bitterly concluded, that there aren't some people who just have a knack of getting by.

While he was at it, Henri Berger had gone to have lunch at the Brasserie de la Gare. The room was certainly big enough to keep two waitresses busy. He recognised André Vasseur's girlfriend straight away, he'd seen her the night before: he went to sit at a table in her row. She was a young woman, about thirty years old, plump but not overly so, with a plump, fresh face; compared to her lover's wife, she could have been described as nondescript were it not for the particular shape of her eyes: she had half-moon eyes, the outer edges lightly falling, eyes which, when she smiled, became a small crescent through which the light of her blue irises glinted, dark enough to be almost violet.

Henri Berger, who had not fallen in love since his youth and thought that it would probably never happen to him again, could well understand why a man could succumb to such eyes: he himself was moved. Instead of the clever predator described by her neighbour, this young woman rather gave him the impression of being just a pleasant girl. The customers called her Isabelle. She responded to them with good spirits and went briskly from one to the other; she seemed to like her work.

As he was tucking into the dish of the day, fried lamb with beans - a little heavy but rather good - the detective wondered what link there could be between the disappearance of Martine Jensen, a bourgeoise of the rich and chic 7th district of Paris and mistress of Boyrive, and a little waitress in an Asnières restaurant.

The hypothesis that he thought of immediately was that Martine had discovered her brother-in-law's liaison and threatened to reveal all to her sister. André Vasseur could have arranged to get rid of her. But the stakes would have had to be very high to get to such a point, for example if he depended financially on his wife, which wasn't the case (Henri Berger had looked into it). VasseurTransEurope was a thriving business that the owner had set up eighteen years earlier, which was to say - long before he met his wife. By the looks of his private car, which must have been worth about seventy-five thousand euros, and by his fleet of lorries of which a good many were new, he didn't seem like the boss of a company that was in dire straits.

One other possibility, since it was accepted that Vasseur was cheating on his wife, was that his sister-in-law had also been his mistress and that, humiliated at being abandoned for someone else, she decided to make his life hell, for example, by blackmailing him for money... Henri Berger didn't believe that either; it didn't gel with what the eldest sister had told him about her sister, that Martine was as rich as her and seemed to have other distractions.

And then to make someone disappear, furthermore a family member, even if you have the logistical means and even the necessary contacts, you have to fit a certain profile: lots of people dream about it, very few are capable of actually doing it. Vasseur was a business man, an established owner; the detective couldn't see him - despite his resemblance to De Niro - getting involved in anything to do with kidnapping or assassination.

On the contrary, supposing that he had wanted to leave his wife, it would have served him well if she heard about his affair via a third party: in general, these are the kinds of things that men don't like to have to announce...

In any case, as long as he didn't see any link to the disappearance of Martine Jensen, it wasn't going to be him who was going to inform his client of the affair: she hadn't hired him to trail her husband and he didn't make a living out of destroying couples).

The fact remained nonetheless that Martine Jensen hadn't been taken by chance. Someone had had a real reason to make her disappear. Henri Berger was inclined to think that she had found out something she shouldn't have, or else that she herself had been the victim of blackmail - a professional matter this time, rather than something personal.

In Latin America, in Asia, in Eastern Europe, kidnappings were becoming more and more frequent: for guerrilla fighters, terrorists, mafia organisations of all kinds it was an easy way of securing funds (the main international companies had even taken out insurance to be able to pay up in the case of a kidnapped employee).

Certainly, in the present case, there had been no ransom demand. But taking a woman from her family could be a means of putting pressure on the road haulier, for example, in order to push him to load up his vehicles with illicit merchandise. Businesses like his were more and more often prey to this kind of coercion. And who knows, wondered the detective, what could be trafficked under the roofs of the vast warehouses of VasseurTransEurope...

As though drawn by a magnet, Henri Berger kicked his heels for the third time around the front gates of André's company. He didn't even bother to hide any more. He'd been there for an hour, in the street, leaning against his car, following the movement of the trucks. He had the feeling that the solution to the problem was right there, inside these depots, and that if he bathed in the atmosphere for long enough, the truth would be transmitted to him as if by osmosis, that an idea would suddenly spring to mind, or that he would end up by discovering something that would get him on track.

At the back of the courtyard, a mechanic was bent over a vehicle's engine, next to his boss, trying to find the cause of an incomprehensible problem in a brand new engine that had just been delivered to them.

"Maybe it's coming from the electric lighting," said André.

"No, I already checked."

"Have you checked if the pump's been drained?"

"It must be that, I'll have a look... hey, he's still there," said the mechanic lifting his head.

"What, who?"

"That bloke there, look. We've seen him about several times. Day before yesterday, when you weren't there, he even came into the courtyard..."

"What did he say?"

"Nothing. He was walking about looking at the lorries, like a real gawper, right, someone who's interested in mechanics."

André had already understood. He walked straight up to the detective.

"Are you looking for something?" he called out, crossing the road.

The detective watched him coming closer, still leaning against his car door.

"Henri Berger," he said, handing over his card, "Private Detective. I was hired by your wife."

"I thought as much. What are you doing here?"

"I'm investigating the disappearance of your sister-in-law, as you know."

"She's paying you a fair bit, my wife is? You're wasting your time, you'll find nothing here."

"Could you give me a minute? I'd like to speak with you."

"Speak to me about what?"

"Ah well, about your sister-in-law of course. Until now, I've only been given one point of view. Maybe you could remember a detail that would give me a lead."

André hesitated. Silently, they weighed each other up.

"Follow me," he finally said, "I can give you fifteen minutes."

He showed the detective into his office, a glass-walled cabin that was raised in the middle of the biggest hanger. From there, he had a panoramic view over the loading of the lorries and onto the courtyard, so much so that everyone could also see what was happening in the office: it was not really the best place for someone who had something to hide.

"What would you like to know?"

Henri Berger got him to describe his sister-in-law, but André Vasseur's judgement of her personality and lifestyle only confirmed what his client had already said, without giving him any new information. One spoke, the other listened, each of them thinking of something else. André wondered if the detective had discovered his affair and if he suspected that his business covered up illegal trafficking, while Berger tried to see through his interlocutor and to discover if he had something other than adultery to hide.

He tried his luck:

"You never had a more... personal relationship with your sister-in-law?"

"What are you insinuating?" said André, throwing him a glare.

"Nothing, leave it. Since Martine Jensen's past hasn't revealed any clues that can help get us anywhere," the detective continued, "I'm starting to wonder if she hadn't been kidnapped by mistake, in someone else's stead, for example, your wife..."

"And why would anyone want to kidnap my wife? What are you thinking?"

"Ah well, Mr Vasseur, have you never been approached by smugglers, these guys who infiltrate legal businesses to use their logistical support systems? International transport businesses are particularly interesting for these kinds of guys..."

"I know that, thank you" André cut him off brusquely and then, lying with aplomb, "I've never been contacted."

"... because when they have it in for a business, these guys won't hesitate to put pressure on it by any means necessary. They're connected to criminal gangs you see, these are very organised guys, very determined... without any scruples."

"No-one has asked me for anything," André lied a second time, "and if traffickers had taken someone in my family to make me obey them, I would have heard about it straight away."

Faced with this perceptive and well-informed man, André congratulated himself that nothing unusual had been going on in his warehouses for a while. In fact, since their interrupted discussion at Boyrive, he'd only carried out two dispatches for Evgueni, the last one at the beginning of August. It had been several weeks, therefore, since the smugglers had shown themselves (maybe they also took holidays?). But André Vasseur foresaw that it wouldn't be long before the freight forwarder showed up again, and if the detective was still there hanging around...

"You don't believe that, without you even knowing it, one of your employees could have fallen into their hands?" the detective proposed.

"You've got it in for my drivers now?"

"One can never be sure."

"Well that would mean that I don't even know what's going on under my own roof... you take me for a fool?"

"Among your drivers," Henri Berger continued, without letting himself be thrown off track, "there's not a bloke with any troubles, any money worries..."

"They've all got money worries."

"Evidently."

"And even if my drivers were involved in trafficking with my lorries, what would that have to do with my sister-in-law? She's never even set foot in here... you're floundering, old boy."

André Vasseur, who had only decided to talk to the detective to get a better idea of what he knew (regarding his love affair, at least, he felt reassured, nothing about the detective's behaviour suggested that he had discovered it), decided to end the interview.

"You'll excuse me if I have to leave you," he said, getting up, "I've got things to do."

They walked down the office stairs together.

"I won't accompany you, you know the way out."

"I'll be fine. Thank you for your cooperation," shouted the detective to him from the courtyard, "I'll come back to see you if I have any questions."

André turned his back on him without responding.

With its imposing white facade, its finely crafted black balconies and its sculpted lintels, the building in which Paula Jensen lived was one of the most beautiful on Saint-Dominique road. 'Quite different to my suburban house in Arcueil,' Henri Berger thought to himself whilst walking into the hall. A large marble staircase, covered with a royal blue carpet, wrapped around the varnished oak elevator - a real museum piece with its glass windows, its mirrors, and its blue velvet bench that coordinated with the stair carpet. He was carried smoothly up to the second floor, and rang at the only door on the whole floor, a large double door of waxed wood, its brass polished daily.

From the moment he stepped through the door, he felt the luxurious comfort of the apartment envelope him. A subtle aroma of ambient jasmine floated in the air, and two Dutch still-life paintings, which looked authentic, decorated the walls away from the glare of the sunlight. A deep woollen carpet muffled his steps.

Paula Jensen walked in front of him into the lounge and planted herself in the middle with a serious expression, without asking him to sit down.

"Do you know why I've asked you to come?" she attacked.

He suggested, "to take stock?"

"Yes. Where are you at?"

The coldness of her welcome broke the affable tone that their relationship had presided under until that point. Henri Berger understood that her husband had given her a talking to.

"I'm getting further forward, Madame, but I still need more time."

"I would say rather that you're not getting anywhere. It's already been ten days."

She had pulled herself up to her full height, copying a very common practice that she must have picked up from her entourage: make one's interlocutors feel guilty in order to destabilise them. Unflappable, the detective waited for what was to come next.

Disconcerted by the lack of reaction, Paula Jensen took a few steps forward on the carpet, joined her hands and opted to shorten the preliminaries.

"Explain to me what you had intended to do at my husband's company?"

"My work."

"I don't understand. What did you think you were going to find there?"

How to explain? For this innocent young woman, managing a business consisted of inviting the chairman and managing director to lunch, signing juicy contracts, giving orders to personnel and sending out extortionate bills. She had no idea of the difficulty of client relations, the brutality of the methods of the competition, the dirty tricks, the dangers. He gave her an evasive response.

"Nothing in particular. I have to cover everything."

"Are you suggesting that my husband could be implicated in my sister's disappearance? How dare you?"

"In business, sometimes things happen without the boss knowing about it... or against their will."

"Please be clearer."

"I've nothing precise to tell you right now. I'm following my instincts."

"Your instincts! Do you understand the effect it could have on his employees, or on his clients, seeing you roaming around his place, surveying his activities as it he was a criminal?"

"It's not like that."

"In any case, it's out of the question that you go back to La Garenne. It won't get you anywhere, it's a waste of time."

"Usually, I decide on how I lead my investigations."

Again, she looked him up and down, thinking she was intimidating him. Evidently, it was with the intention of intimidating him that instead of coming to his office she'd called him to her apartment, this superb apartment which she'd come by effortlessly, merely by being born, on the second floor where traditionally only the nobility lived, in an early-20th century building built expressly to impress its visitors. In the informed eyes of

Henri Berger, this inelegant and naive way of boasting about the riches that surrounded her in order to impress him denoted, rather, a sort of insecurity.

"Ah well," she replied dryly, "you are going to have to decide on something else."

"If you don't permit me to lead my investigation as I see fit, I will be forced to give up pursuing it," Berger announced without losing his cool.

"What! You're threatening to quit...?"

"I'm not threatening you. But you have understood."

Thus, instead of finding relief by passing the stinging reprimand that her husband had given her onto the detective, and of receiving his apologies, it was in fact he who had turned it back on her... She was stupefied and outraged.

"You're jumping on the first pretext to mask your incompetence," she threw back at him in a bitter tone, "You can't find anything, so there we go. You're fumbling about. You don't know where to look anymore."

"If that's what you think," said the detective, vexed, "well then we'd best leave it there."

"I was going to say it myself. Send me the bill!"

"Your down payment will be fine. I will send you a settled invoice." He bowed towards her, "Madame..." and then moved towards the door.

"Thank God!" he heard her exclaim behind him, "It's still dearly paid looking at your results!"

The proverbial straw... Suddenly, Henri Berger had had enough of being mistreated by this family, firstly by the husband and then by this young ignorant and imperious woman. He turned.

"Go and see what your husband is doing at 14 Paul-Eluard street, in Asnières. Then you'll see if I haven't found anything!" And he left.

Disregarding the extravagantly-decorated lift, he went back down the two floors four steps at a time. Deep down, although he had been humiliated, he wasn't unhappy to be rid of the whole affair. If what he'd felt instinctively was right, Martine Jensen had been killed, and there wasn't any more that could be done for her. As for him, at fifty-three years old, he couldn't see himself confronting a network of smugglers and drug traffickers alone. Throwing a spanner in the works of the mafia just to amuse himself! His house was nearly paid off, if everything went well, he still had a good few years ahead of him. It wasn't a good time for him to get himself stupidly killed. As the singer Alain Souchon said, "Life is worth nothing, but nothing is worth life."

The following Friday, Paula told her husband that she was going to spend the weekend at Boyrive. He thought it was a good idea, it would do her some good to have some fresh air, and he advised her, since the weather forecast was good, to take some jogging gear and to go for a run for a few kilometers. He himself had work to catch up on and would be busy the whole day Saturday on Balzac road, but he'd do everything he could to join her by Sunday morning.

The next day, André went early to his office in order to write some urgent letters. At half twelve, his correspondence done, he put the letters next to his secretary's computer so that she could swiftly write them up on Monday, and then left the building whistling. The weather forecast hadn't been wrong: for an October month, it was absolutely splendid weather, warm and sunny - an Indian summer. He got into his car, made a u-turn at the Place de l'Etoile and turned into the Avenue de la Grande Armée. En route, he stopped by Lenôtre, coming out ten minutes later loaded with provisions, and set off in the direction of Asnières.

"I told you not to bring anything," Isabelle reminded him, seeing him come with the trademark bag, "I've already prepared lunch."

An appetising smell filled the small house. André planted a kiss on the young woman's cheek and lifted up the boy who was already hanging off his legs.

"But what do we have here?!" he said, shaking him for an instant in the air at arms' length, "It's Leo! Leo the little devil!" and he popped him back on the floor.

"That smells good. What are we having?"

"Roasted veal with pearl onions. Take off your jacket, it's nearly ready."

She popped her son down at the table and sat opposite him.

"So, you have a day off today?" said André, while she fed the child.

"It's my turn, you know that."

With her colleague at the Brasserie de la Gare, they arranged to work each Saturday in turn. The majority of their clientele comprised the workers from the surrounding areas, and the restaurant was full to the brim on work days. On Saturdays they only needed one waitress, and the restaurant was closed Sundays.

"I've the whole weekend free," added Isabelle, though she didn't dare ask her lover if he was intending to spend it with her.

"How's work going?" André asked her mechanically.

He had met her at the Brasserie, one day when he'd gone in by chance to have a quick lunch between two appointments. He'd sat at one of her tables and immediately something had passed between them. While waiting on him, she couldn't stop smiling; she even smiled at him from afar while serving other customers. As for André, he couldn't stop himself from looking at her eyes, her fairy eyes like a crescent moon... she wasn't tall, maybe a little chubby, but with a pretty and solid body, shapely arms and legs with delicate wrists and ankles. This was far worse than just falling head over heels, André felt like he knew her, as if she were the embodiment of something he'd always been looking for.

After a few weeks, thanks to her, he felt so in tune with life, he felt such richness, that he was already dreaming of a divorce. He liked Paula, he appreciated her qualities, but she wasn't really his wife. With time, their relationship had grown cold and he had started to tell himself that it would be better to leave her while she was still young and beautiful and had every chance of meeting a man who would make her happy. A first marriage is often a failure and thank God they didn't have any children, a child would only have suffered as a result.

He prepared to tell her that he'd met someone, to begin discussing a separation, when the Russian mafia fell on him, and he suddenly had to deal with this enormous problem which meant that his personal worries had to take a backseat. And then his sister-in-law disappeared, plunging his wife into a profound distress, and there was no further question of André inflicting any further pain on her.

Furthermore, why should anyone be forced to 'choose', to hurt someone? No-one can imagine how difficult it is for a man. Isabelle was discreet, she asked for nothing. As for him, he didn't feel so bad having two households, he even found a certain equilibrium that way...

"Work's okay," Isabelle responded, "but the customers can be a real pain in the neck sometimes."

In the beginning, André had suggested that she leave her job: he didn't like seeing her wearing herself out for a pathetic salary, he felt like he was taking advantage of her. But Isabelle was fond of her job, and of what she called her independence. And now he almost felt happy with it: it gave their relationship dignity. He respected her.

"... their steaks are over-cooked, under-cooked, the wine's corked, some even have the nerve to send their food back! They're not at Maxim's, right?!" She lifted the lid of the casserole dish, basted the roast, and returned to looking after her son.

As well as everything else, she was a wonderful cook, something André always thought was a good sign in a woman. Above all, he felt good with her. As long as he was in her three-room house, he forgot his difficulties, this band of Muscovite traffickers whose hooks he'd been stupid enough to get snared on, his worry about the imminent return of Evgueni...

Isabelle got her little boy to swallow a last spoonful of puree, and picked him up out of his chair.

"Now we're going to sleepy-byes," she said. "I'm going to put him to bed. Can you lay the table while you're waiting? There's a tomato salad in the fridge."

Their meal finished, it was still a beautiful day outside and André suggested they go and sit in the sun. Isabelle liked the idea; if he hadn't suggested they 'go and have a siesta,' it meant that he was intending to spend the night with her.

It wasn't quite four o'clock when the tenant at 12, rue Paul-Eluard (the widow of the county employee that the detective had come to question a few days earlier), who was on the lawn watering her begonias, remarked that another big car was parking behind the BMW, which was stopped in front of number 14. She put down her watering can, while the retired gentleman at number eight, busy with trimming his hedge, also froze, the cutter in the air. Both of them followed with their eyes the elegant young blond who was getting out of the car and crossing the road with a determined step. They lifted up their heads and lay in wait, expecting to hear a rumpus.

Paula didn't even need to ring the bell. Beyond the gate, not a meter away, in the middle of a garden as big as a handkerchief, her husband lounged in a deckchair, happy as a suburbanite on a summer's day. Nearby, a young woman kneeling on the grass played with a child. For the length of a demi-second, Paula and André's eyes met, and just as quickly Paula left, running to her car. The clack of a car door was heard and the 508 revved into life. The whole thing hadn't lasted more than two minutes. Peace once more fell on Paul-Eluard street. Disappointed, the neighbours went back to the gardening.

André's heart beat fast enough to burst. Thankfully, Isabelle, whose back was to the gate at that moment, hadn't seen anything. She'd hardly moved her head when hearing a car engine roaring and getting into gear. He got up and went to get himself a beer in the kitchen.

"You're already drinking?" she said surprised, seeing him come back with his glass.

André sat back down on his deckchair. First, he must calm down. Nothing was urgent, he knew that Paula wasn't going to go back to Saint-Dominique road. Usually, when they had a serious argument, she would flee to Boyrive or even stay at the Hotel Lutetia, a few doors down from their place. He guessed who had told his wife: that bastard detective! And he hadn't even been asked to do so! André knew his wife was too proud and too prudent to have her husband followed. His eyes fell on Isabelle, on all fours on the grass, still playing 'little trains' with her son. She asked him, without turning around,

"What do you want to eat tonight?"

"I can't stay," said André.

"Oh, okay," she said sadly.

André felt ridiculous and guilty. He didn't know any more if he was living in a drama or a comedy. For a while now, calamities had hit him like hail: the Muscovite smugglers, the disappearance of his sister-in-law, and to top it all off, his affair discovered by his wife... suddenly he felt struck by a huge blow and fell asleep.

Three hours later, back on Saint-Dominique road, he called the Hotel Lutetia: Paula wasn't there. He asked them to get her to call him back if she turned up. Then he called Boyrive. Thinking his wife would be calmer if she knew he was home, he left a message on the answering machine: "I'm at the flat, I'm waiting for you. Don't worry too much about earlier, it's not what you think..." Pronouncing these words, that Paula was maybe listening to beside the phone without picking up, André didn't think he was very convincing.

The morning post waited for him on the lounge table, and he went to examine it. The never-ending bills, mail adverts, invitations to society events which they hadn't been going to for two months... An envelope was addressed to him personally. He opened it. It was a summons from the Customs Information and Enquiries Bureau: Counter-Forgeries Department, for Tuesday 22nd October at nine o'clock, which was to say in three days time.

André dropped into a chair, knocked out and down for the count.

CHAPTER 8.

On the appointed day, with two copies of the summons in hand (one had been sent to the company headquarters), André presented himself at the counter-forgeries department of the CIEB, on the Charonne road in the eleventh district of Paris. The summons were signed by Jean Baldayan, Director of the Anti-Fraud department.

Though he tried to appear unruffled, André felt ill at ease. Thanks to a basic knowledge of the law which he'd acquired during his studies, he knew that if the customs officers thought it useful for their enquiry he could be handed over to the police and remanded in custody on the basis of nothing more than a simple suspicion, which could be legally prolonged to four days in very serious cases (and God only knows if illegal trafficking and associating with smugglers fit into this category). Not knowing when he'd get out, and in order to face the customs officials in the best possible shape he could, he'd gotten up early, made himself do quarter of an hour of gym exercises (push-ups and weights) and had eaten a solid breakfast, enough to stop him from feeling hungry for the whole day. Then he dressed warmly in clothes appropriate for the circumstances: a sports jacket and a fleece jumper (gear that, in his profession, was perfectly normal even for the boss), trousers that were a little too small and fit snugly around the waist so they stayed up without a belt, a comfortable pair of moccasins that meant, if need be, he wouldn't have to drag his heels in shoes without laces. He'd decided not to take any toiletries so as not to give the impression that he was expecting to be detained, which could be interpreted as a confession. A few months earlier, during a business lunch, André had found out that certain major companies were organising courses on 'being remanded in custody' for their managers. At the time it had given him a good laugh; today he regretted not having been able to participate.

Since the previous Saturday, when Paula had surprised him in Isabelle's garden and their eyes had briefly met (he could still see her horrified look), she hadn't given him any sign of life. He had checked several times and she wasn't at the Lutetia Hotel, and she wasn't responding to any messages he had left at the house in Boyrive either. Before leaving the apartment, he'd left a note on the desk and then telephoned Boyrive one last time to let her know where he was.

After making him wait for twenty minutes in a corridor buffeted by gusts of wind and patrolled by uniformed customs officials with a military step, he was shown him into a large room furnished with two desks. Only the one at the back was manned. A man sat there, his back to the window, where he seemed absorbed in intensely scrutinising a thick file. He welcomed his visitor with a dry "Good day, Monsieur" and ordered André to sit. André complied.

"You are André Vasseur, CEO of VasseurTransEurope Limited," he said without lifting his gaze. "What year was the company founded?"

"1991" said André.

"Capital stock?"

"One million francs. One hundred and fifty thousand euros."

"How was it set up?"

"It's a family business. I own seventy-nine percent of the shares myself, my father owns fifteen percent; the remaining six percent belong to a third party, a friend."

"How many employees?"

"Thirty-four. The drivers, the mechanics, and the office: accounting and secretariat."

"Are you satisfied?"

"With what?" asked André.

"With your results. It's a burgeoning business?"

"It's going well. I started in 1991 with three leased vehicles. My fleet has grown to twenty-four lorries today."

"Of course, the single market, the opening of the borders..." the customs officer commented in a nostalgic but slightly disapproving tone.

With his nose still buried in his papers, he recommenced his questioning in a monotonous tone of voice. André had the impression that the Director already knew as much as he did, and that he was simply getting him to reconfirm the details that were in the files: turnover, names of his major clients, destinations of exports, frequency...

Suddenly the official lifted his head: two black, piercing eyes burrowed into Andrés'.

"Do you know the name Evgueni Voronkovitch?"

He had a thin face, almost middle-eastern, with dark black hair flattened onto a bony skull, a hooked nose, and deep-set eyes under bushy eyebrows (although he spoke French without trace of an accent, one could have supposed he was of Turkish or Iranian origin). The expression of this man who, in some way was the representative face of Customs, the Inland Revenue and the Police all at once, seemed rather glacial.

André held his stare nevertheless.

"He's a freight forwarder," he said, "one of my clients. Well, he represents three of my clients."

"Since when and for how long?"

"Nearly a year. He works for two companies in Moscow and one in Tallinn."

"These Russian and Estonian clients, you've never seen them of course?"

"No," said André, "but the shipments are perfectly organised and all the documents are in order. Mr Voronkovitch is an efficient and competent professional."

The customs official made him explain at length the terms of their collaboration and the detail of the services provided by the road haulier; André explained them to him without becoming impatient.

"I've never had serious problems with these clients," he declared, "I told you, the trajectories of the shipments are well organised and payments are made punctually. The terms of the contract have always been upheld."

"Slow down a minute there," exclaimed the other, "anything to the contrary would be surprising!" and once again his black eyes bored into him.

André, who had decided to say as little as possible, settled for fixing his interlocutor with a well-placed, quizzical look.

"You do realise," Baldayan continued, "that smugglers regularly infiltrate ordinary companies in order to cover up their activities, and that road haulage companies, businesses like yours, are particularly appealing to them?"

"Of course," responded André, "In the industry we talk about it between ourselves, we're looking at developing ways of protecting our businesses. Our union has already organised two conferences on the subject."

"We call it the 'cuckoo's strategy'. You know, the bird that lays its eggs in other birds' nests..."

"Oh?" said André, "I didn't know that."

He had started to realise that the customs official didn't have anything against him personally and he felt somewhat reassured. The last export that he'd done for Evgueni was dated the 8th August that year - a supposed shipment of 'small Chinese furniture items' to Poland (he didn't have the faintest idea what was actually in the container). That was two and a half months ago. If customs had checked one of his lorries on the road or at a border post and discovered illicit cargo, he would have heard about it soon enough. He hadn't, therefore, been summoned in connection to a particular issue of smuggled goods. Maybe VasseurTransEurope had been flagged on the CIS, the European customs information system which collected and checked millions of pieces of information? If that was the case, it was annoying: it meant that his company was being watched, but it was better than a blatant offence. Or maybe they had questioned Evgueni and he'd talked about him, or they'd found André's details in Evgueni's address book...

"Fortunately, there's a lot of us," continued André, "it's a very fragmented sector. We won't all be affected."

"But your company is particularly vulnerable. Because of its longevity, its respectability, and its work in the luxury goods industry... you've never noticed anything unusual in the cargo that Mr Voronkovitch had you transport?"

"Never. I can't keep an eye on everything, of course - I've got a lot of other clients. But all the documents are overseen by my office and I often check them myself. We've never noticed any irregularities in the paperwork."

"And the containers, do you ever check them?"

"Rarely. It's not easy to open them. And we don't have any particular reason to mistrust Mr Voronkovitch."

"Evgueni was arrested on 14th August," Baldayan announced brutally, fixing André at the same time with a penetrating glare in order to gauge his reaction: fear or relief?

André's heart leaped in his chest, but he managed to remain unperturbed. It was fortunate he wasn't attached to a lie detector.

""Oh," he said stupidly, "that's why you've brought me here."

The customs official closed the open file in front of him with a sharp click.

"Just some simple questions," he said, "for the moment. Right, we'll leave it there for today. Send me a complete file of documents corresponding to the shipments that you've made for your freight forwarder, and then the bank statements for your company for the last three years. You have one week. That will be all. Good day, Monsieur."

Coming out of the building, André breathed in the pollution of the Charonne road as though it was a breath of fresh air. He walked into the first café he passed and ordered a double espresso at the counter. He felt a kind of animal joy, exultation even. The clinking of the glasses and saucers on the counter surface, the comings and goings of customers, the jokes and exclamations of a group of students from the art school nearby, everything seemed alive, full of meaning, and familiar. It's surprising how the most ordinary gestures, simple everyday pleasures, suddenly seem of huge value when you are afraid of losing them. In fact, during the two hours that he spent on the witness stand, he'd never thought that they'd let him go so easily.

He knew now that Evgueni's arrest had led the customs officials to him. But how they'd managed to find Evgueni was a mystery. André couldn't be his only haulier, and customs must have gotten hold of another of Evgueni's cargo loads. It was easy to understand that the freight forwarder was, for them, a very interesting catch because his activities placed him at the very centre of the smugglers' activities, and being the relay man he was therefore in direct contact with the heads of the network. Thanks to him, the customs investigators could hope to pin down those at the top of the web, which interested them much more than just seizing smuggled goods. And André told himself he'd had a real stroke of luck: if customs were directing their efforts towards the head honchos, there was no reason that they'd be interested in probing especially deeply into his affairs.

He knocked back his coffee and went back to his car to head over to La Garenne where long hours of work awaited him: a renegotiation with a difficult client, a driver lost somewhere in Spain, never-ending formalities... the usual. At least he was certain that Evgueni wouldn't come to bother him again.

Worn out by this trying day, André went home early. He put his car in the garage and went on foot to the Bac Road. He was hungry. Not for one of these light suppers that the maid would prepare for him when Paula wasn't there and that he only had to reheat in the microwave. He was hungry for a big, fat, invigorating meal, with good hearty food. André wasn't a man to use alcohol to beat stress.

On Bac Road, he went into the local deli. Imagining the insipid sandwich that would probably have been handed over to him if he'd been remanded in custody, he bought himself a beautiful slice of wild boar paté, a big portion of Flemish endives, and a gorgeous morsel of Brittany prune flan. He'd been living life as a singleton for three days now, and generally he preferred family life - no doubt because he'd had a happy childhood with his parents - but he wasn't unhappy with his solitude, which gave him some peace and silence at a time when he most needed to concentrate on things.

Arriving home, he put the endives in the oven, set the table in the kitchen and poured himself a glass of wine from the bottle opened the day before. Once he'd finished his meal, he went into the lounge and settled into his favourite armchair, a glass of cognac in hand. He had the whole evening ahead of him to take stock of the situation and get his thoughts into order.

Thinking about it, the customs summons wasn't so alarming. There had been no evidence of any criminal offence, and whatever happened, André would stubbornly maintain that he believed he was transporting cargo as described on the documents and no-one could prove anything to the contrary (fortunately, Baldayan seemed to be totally unaware of the clandestine package dropped off in Milan by one of his drivers). Furthermore, André had a good reputation. No police record. His business was going well. He had no money worries for the moment and he was married to a woman who was very well-off. The payment for the services rendered to Evgueni weren't out of the ordinary, and he had no foreign bank accounts where he could accumulate concealed cash payments. Certainly, when they examined the documents given by Evgueni, the customs officials would be quick to notice that the stamps were forged, but if the border post controllers hadn't noticed anything, then they couldn't reproach a simple road haulier for being taken in by them. There was even a bright side to the whole thing: now that Customs had an eye on him, he could predict that his shipments would be regularly checked and suddenly his business would lose all interest for the traffickers: in their eyes, his cover was blown. The first wave of fear ebbing away, André saw that in reality he didn't risk losing much. At the very worst, he might be subjected to a painful tax audit.

But there was something more serious than that. He was now certain that there was a link between his sister-in-law's kidnapping and the Russian mafia: he'd had a sudden presentiment when Baldayan had told him about Evgueni's arrest. He'd been arrested on the 14th August; Martine had disappeared on the 21st, one week later. And then André thought of their encounter, the day when, on Evgueni's orders, he'd organised a discreet meeting at Boyrive, and Martine had opened the door of the study at the very moment that the lid of the two briefcases had been lifted, leaving their bags of cocaine and bundles of money for all to see.

Furious at this intrusion, his visitors had quickly left the room, but it was easy to imagine what had followed. Evgueni had gone and told his boss that he'd been surprised and they'd simply decided to cease using André's services for drug trafficking, settling for making him transport their contrebande as usual.

But everything had changed when Evgueni had been arrested. Suddenly, his bosses were afraid. Evgueni was at the heart of the organisation: he was an important man, polyglot and smart, accustomed to the work that they got him to do. He knew all the resources and all of the traps, and by very virtue of his role he was in regular contact with the big shots of the network, and was in the know about too many things. He knew names, faces, addresses... Evgueni's bosses had thought that from him it wouldn't be long before customs and the police arrived at VasseurTransEurope's doorstep, and they remembered the sister-in-law who'd surprised Evgueni with a briefcase of coke. The investigators might find out about her when questioning the road haulier, and then Evgueni would be really exposed... Drugs were on a completely different level to smuggled goods. Unmasked, Evgueni faced a heavy sentence, and could be tempted to make a deal with the police to reveal information in exchange for something lighter. André himself didn't worry them: it was in his interest to keep quiet. But his young sister-in-law wouldn't hesitate before telling the police what she'd seen when they came to question her. And the bigwigs had thought it more prudent to erase her. Instead of killing her there and then, in the Boyrive forest where she was walking with her dog, they preferred to kidnap her, which was less obvious and would hold up the police enquiry. But André was in no doubt that Martine had been murdered. It had been two months since she'd disappeared and there was no chance that the mafia would have burdened themselves for so long with a dangerous witness. The saddest, most absurd thing of all, was that she hadn't even noticed the compromising briefcases - she had died for nothing.

It was for this death, and for the sadness and pain of his wife, that André held himself responsible: his carelessness and stupidity had caused a big mess. From that point forward, it was clear what he had to do. He'd already behaved like a fool, he wouldn't now behave like a goddamn son of a bitch.

He hadn't touched his cognac. He took the glass back to the kitchen and went to bed.

The next day, like every Wednesday as long as there were no major obstacles, André left the office at five-thirty and went to Asnières where Isabelle awaited him. She'd dolled herself up, and he knew she'd done it especially for him since they never went out on a weekday. In fact, even on a weekend, they rarely went out together. Whenever they did, they went to a restaurant that was out-of-the-way, where there was no risk of André being recognised, and even then he didn't feel at ease. Four or five times, he'd taken her to the cinema, but really it was to make her happy, because for him, the cinema - well...

Today she wore a tight skirt and a little clear-grey crew neck jumper, cashmere, which clung to her ravishing chest; its short sleeves showing off her pretty arms. As André had said he liked it when a woman was feminine, she'd put on her high-heeled court shoes and seamed stockings. Her mid-length chestnut hair, thick and shining, framed her lightly made-up face, which lit up with joy at seeing him. André looked at her smiling eyes, her bewitching half-moon eyes, with wonder, as if seeing them for the first time - maybe because he knew that it was the last.

Léo ran towards him, followed by his mother. He hugged them both together for a moment.

"Get yourself comfortable," said Isbaelle, "I'll finish sorting out the little one. You want an aperitif while you're waiting?"

"A beer'll be fine," said André, sitting down heavily on the imitation leather sofa.

"You're not taking off your jacket? You seem worried tonight. Something niggling you?"

He took a deep breath and launched in.

"I've got something to tell you. We have to have a serious talk."

"What about? What do you want to tell me?"

215

"It's about my wife."

The smile that had brightened Isabelle's face vanished. She turned to him with a worried expression.

"Something bad's happened, something really bad," André continued, "Paula's sister is dead."

"When did that happen?"

He improvised with an effort.

"... Sunday." This was torture: indirectly responsible for an assassination, resolved to renounce the woman he loved, the drama of his life obliged him to make up fibs, lies and half-truths, like a fickle husband in a bedroom farce.

"What happened?"

"She had an accident... a car accident. She was killed instantly. My wife adored her sister, she's very depressed. I can't leave her now, you understand?"

"But I never asked you to leave her."

"It's my duty to stay with her."

"So stay with her," said Isabelle, "what's stopping you? We can keep going just as we are."

"Continuing as we are isn't a life. Especially for you... You're young," he began again, congratulating himself on never having told her that he'd dreamed for a moment of getting a divorce in order to marry her, "you should have a man who looks after you, a man who's totally yours."

"But I'm fine as I am," said Isabelle, "I don't ask for anything more."

"You should think of your future. You've got to build your own life, have a real family."

"You want to get rid of me, is that it? You don't love me any more?"

"Of course I do - don't..." André broke in hurriedly, embarrassed. He took a few swigs of beer, then added, "there's something else. My wife knows about us."

"How did she find out?"

"Someone told her. And she followed me, she saw my car in front of your house. She even saw me in the garden."

Isabelle turned very pale. Silently, she went to put her son in amongst his toys.

"Come here," said André, "come sit here close to me."

Instead of complying, Isabelle came back and planted herself in front of him, worried and on guard.

"When did she come?" she asked.

"Last Saturday."

"Well, I didn't see her."

"You were playing with Léo, you were looking elsewhere. It happened very quickly. She didn't say a thing and just left."

"So, we're finished, the two of us? That's what you wanted to tell me?"

"I think it would be better that we don't see each other for a while."

"Tell me straight that you want to break it off," Isabelle cried out, tears beginning to run down her cheeks.

"Come here," repeated André, patting the sofa.

This time, in tears, she decided to join him. He pulled her into his arms and started to talk softly and slowly, assuring her that he still loved her, that he'd miss her, it would be very painful for him to be separated from her... snuggled in his arms, Isabelle sobbed loudly while she fiddled with her handkerchief.

André quickly realised that little Léo had stopped playing and that his eyes were fixed on them, filled with distress. A wave of guilt came over him.

"Listen," he said, filled with sudden inspiration, "I don't want to leave you like this. I'm going to buy you a flat. You remember the block that's being built next to the school? Would you like to live there? A pretty apartment right next to the school, Léo wouldn't even have to cross the road to get there... What do you say? That would be nice, right? You and your son would have nothing to worry about for the years ahead, and I would know that you were safe. The block will soon be finished, we'll do the paperwork and in a few months, in Spring next year at the latest, you'll be settled in your new apartment..."

Isabelle had stopped crying, she was dabbing her eyes with a tissue.

"So," she said, "we'll see each other again?"

Going back to his place a few hours later (break-up scenes can be very long, especially between two people who love each other and don't want to leave one another's company), while walking into the entrance, he heard a noise, distant but distinct, at the end of the corridor. He went to check: a ray of light shone from under his sister-in-law's bedroom door, her childhood bedroom, which she'd kept and occasionally came back to sleep in. André approached the door and knocked gently; not getting any response, he half-opened the door. Paula was lain out on the bed, her face hidden behind an open book.

"Ah, you're there, you've come back... errr, evening my darling."

She emitted a muffled growl, and turned sharply away from him towards the wall.

André didn't insist. He softly closed the door and went into the main bedroom. His heart was filled with shame and pity. His unhappy wife would never know what had happened to her sister. He couldn't tell anyone what he'd understood about her kidnapping (and moreover he had no way of proving anything) and Martine Jensen's disappearance would join the multitude of open cases, the millions of disappearances that are never solved. Paula would realise, little by little, that she would never see her sister again, and he would have to live the rest of his life with his secret and his remorse. The only thing to do at present, in order to try and atone for what he had done and so as to forgive himself a little, was to carry out his resolution and dedicate himself to his wife until the end of his days, to make her as happy as he possibly could.

The next morning at seven o'clock, André, who was crossing the corridor to go and make himself some coffee, noticed his wife through the half-opened door to the lounge. She was sat at her desk, made-up, hair done, dressed from head to toe. Hesitant, he stepped over the threshold and went forward a few paces.

"Hello..."

"Hello."

"What're you up to, you going out?"

"No. I'm sorting some paperwork."

He started to turn to leave.

"We have to talk," said Paula.

"If you like," responded André, who would have like to avoid it but didn't see how he could get away.

She got up from the desk and went to sit in the middle of the large sofa. Observing the ceremony of the occasion, André sat in a chair opposite her.

"Well," she annouced, "I've decided that we should get a divorce."

"But - no," said André.

"What do you mean, no?" In a firm tone, belied by her uncertain and unhappy gaze, she added seriously "given the circumstances, I think it's better that we separate. There's no other solution."

"Come on darling, we're not going to get divorced over something so trivial."

"Trivial? But you've gone and had a family!"

"What," said André, "what family?"

"But... you have a child! I saw him!"

"Of course not, what were you thinking? The child that you saw is nearly four years old, and I met his mother a few... not long ago."

"How long?"

"Eeerrr... three or four months."

"You've been cheating on me for four months!"

"I'm not cheating on you. I didn't think it was going to last so long, but it made me feel bad, this girl, all alone with her kid..." he added "you know, it was out of pity."

He wasn't proud of disowning Isabelle, lying to one, lying to the other. How stupid was this Western civilisation where a man was forbidden to have several companions, where if he was attached to two women, he was forced to sacrifice one. He couldn't have asked for more in the world than to be able to look after both of them, Paula as well as Isabelle...

"That was why you were working those 'weekends at the office.'"

"But I was at the office. Most of the time, I was working."

"How did you meet her?"

"In a restaurant where she works."

"As a waitress?"

"That's right."

"I've had my husband stolen by a waitress!" exclaimed Paula with disdain, that haughty upper class arrogance that he had always disliked about her.

André found an acceptable explanation.

"It was at a point when I felt you were pulling away from me. I felt alone."

"I never pulled away from you," lied Paula in turn, "what an idea. It was you, rather, who was pulling away."

"I will never see this person again, I promise," said André, trying to cut a long story short, beginning to think of the client that he should be seeing at nine am at La Garenne.

"You were like a pasha in his little garden!"

"I was relaxing, that's all. I'm tired at the moment. I've had some serious trouble at work."

"You should have talked to me about it. You never talk to me about anything."

"You couldn't have done anything. It would only have worried you. But right now, things are going much better, I can tell you. My problems have been dealt with once and for all. I can see the light at the end of the tunnel."

"I thought that you wanted to leave me, to get a divorce," said Paula in a crushed voice. She contemplated her unhappiness, which she expressed in her restrained manner, "to lose my sister and my husband all at the same time..."

André left his armchair to come closer to her and, repeating the gesture that he'd given his mistress twelve hours earlier, he wrapped his arm around his wife.

"You're crazy! Divorce you? The idea never even came into my mind. I will never leave you, I swear."

Moved by his own words, and since she'd laid her head on his shoulder, he placed a kiss on her silky hair, her beautiful hair so delicately perfumed by an expensive lotion.

"I've got to go," he said, "my first meeting is at nine am and I've got to look over the file beforehand."

"You'll be back late?"

"No, I'll come home early."

Then remembering his promise to be more available and attentive from that moment on, he bravely suggested "we could continue this conversation, if you like."

Once her husband had gone, Paula stayed there for a long time, pensive. Finally, as if she had a feeling that time would inevitably confine Martine to oblivion, Paula went to find her sister's photo in the silver frame that she'd given her for her last birthday, and placed it in plain sight on the chimney mantelpiece in the lounge. It was a portrait done by the renowned Harcourt Studio in Paris, which Martine had had taken one day to amuse herself, a grainy 1950's vintage starlet photo. Its anachronism already seemed to consign her to the past.

Epilogue

A few weeks later in Le Havre an early-riser who was walking along the coastline noticed a strange, voluminous object down below. Probably washed in at high tide, it had then got stuck between the rocks when the sea had pulled back. Intrigued, he took the narrow path that went down to the beach. He didn't have to go far before realising that the object was a human corpse. Deciding not to go any closer, he turned on his phone and called the Gendarmerie.

That same day, late morning, having learnt of the discovery of a woman's body that had washed ashore on the Le Havre coast just nearby, one of the two Rouen gendarmes, who had taken around the photo of Martine Jensen in Rouen at the request of their Neuville colleagues after her credit card had been used in several shops, notified Brigadier Chief Gallard of what was happening. Gallard immediately called Paula Vasseur in her Parisian residence and asked her to go to the coroner's office in Le Havre, where the corpse had been taken, in order to see if it was her sister.

Paula and her husband presented themselves at the Institute at four o'clock sharp. When she entered the laboratory, Paula had a brief moment of hope: the obese body hidden under the sheet couldn't be Martine, who had been a slim and slender young woman. But, having asked to her to come nearer, the forensic scientist folded the sheet back off the head and Paula recognised her sister's blond hair (or what remained of it), a rare Nordic blond, which they both got from their father. And then the height of the body was correct: one meter seventy five, stated the medical examiner who had measured it. He made as if to fold the sheet back further.

"May I? She had some distinctive marks on her stomach that could help to identify her..."

With the body completely uncovered, Paula discerned a tattoo that her sister had had done near the belly-button to a design that she'd drawn herself, of which only a few dots of scattered ink remained on her distended belly, swollen during the long time it had spent in the water. Paula put her hand to her mouth and collapsed.

While the doctor and her assistant tried to revive her, the Brigadier Chief took André aside.

"Your sister-in-law didn't drown," he said, "she was killed by a bullet, a bullet in the nape of the neck. According to the preliminary observations of the forensics, there was no act of violence, no torture, her skin doesn't bear any marks of ill-treatment. And, although it's as far as they can tell, what with the state the body was found in, she wasn't raped either..."

André nodded his head without saying a word.

"A clean and neat piece of work. A real execution."

And as André was still silent,

"It was a carefully thought out act," continued the Brigadier, "it rather makes one think of a settling of scores. Maybe your sister-in-law was mixed up in something shady. A drugs deal, for example: it's quite common these days. But I don't really think so. I rather think that she was witness to something that she shouldn't have seen," and the Brigadier added, looking at André with an inquisitive and severe gaze, "something serious and compromising."

André blinked. The gendarme had hit the bull's eye and seemed to suspect him.

"Do you have any idea of what it could be?"

"None," responded André in a heavy voice, hoping that his confusion would be credited to the painful circumstances he and his wife found themselves in.

"Well," concluded the Brigadier, "now that the corpse has been found, the police will open an enquiry. And believe me, they won't go easy on whoever has done this."

Driving back to Paris, his wife weeping silent tears by his side, André thought about what was going to happen from that moment. Inevitably, he would be the first to be suspected. The police aren't idiots and are aware of the amount of trafficking that the transport industry can cover up. He would have to undergo a ruthless investigation of his company. One clear morning, they would come in by the dozens, minutely examining his lorries, questioning his drivers. He himself would be summoned to the police station and questioned at length. Sooner or later, he would reveal to the investigators what had happened: the pressure of the Russian smugglers that weighed on him, forcing him and his lorries, on pain of death, to commit illegal and criminal acts. He would reveal the villainous meeting that he'd had the stupidity to organise in Boyrive, for fear of reprisals, and the way in which, unfortunately, his young sister-in-law had half-opened the study door at the very moment that the case filled with cocaine was open, as well as the suitcase that contained the stacks of banknotes, which had made the Mafioso's think that she'd seen something and, for their own security, had finally led them to kidnap her and eliminate her.

Yes, André clearly saw what was going to happen, everything that he was going to have to tell the police officers, and the consequences that his confession would have for himself. And, strangely, it didn't frighten him anymore. Deep down, he knew that it would do him some good to let out the heavy secret that had been his alone to carry for several months.

It would even be a huge relief.

Original registered at:

Société des Gens de Lettres – Paris
INPI – Paris
Copyright France

www.ingramcontent.com/pod-product-compliance
Lightning Source LLC
Chambersburg PA
CBHW051129020726
47501CB00005B/1425